Scandal
In
The Family

Scandal
In
The Family

Errol Samuel

To my mother and father...

Prologue

The Beginning

It was hurricane season, and all night long the lightning and thunder battled on the hill tops of the small island in the southern Caribbean Sea, Grenada. The rain falling on the galvanized roof of the wooden house, sounded like chants from a football stadium. It was as if each sheet of galvanized carried a different note, just like a steel pan. The sun burst through the dark clouds, stretching its beam of light, like a giant waking up to take the morning shift. The sound of war gave way to birds chatting to each other in their beautiful singing language, as they gathered breakfast for their young ones.

Yet this was no ordinary morning, for it was the day of the funeral of Mrs Johnson. Her husband had passed a few years earlier and tragedy once again revisited the family, this time taking the mother and leaving six children to fend for themselves. As it was in those days, the older children took charge and the elderly people in the village kept their eyes out for them.

Bee was the youngest of Mrs Johnson's children. She had been very close to her mother, so her mother's death was very difficult to accept. Her mother had gone on a long journey, never to return. She would no longer be singing and cooking, and baking her cakes and bread to sell in the village and at the market.

About midday some of the neighbours came to the house to make sure all the children were dressed and ready. The older ones helped the younger ones. Very little was said between the siblings that Sunday; each child reflected on the loss of their mother in their own way. Bee had hardly spoken a word since they took her beloved mother away, praying for her to hurry up and come back home.

The cemetery was just outside the village, nestled beside the church. Bee and her brothers and sisters walked solemnly down the road. The villagers walked alongside them in a procession. Some hummed hymns. Some shed a tear. This was one of their own. The village was really like a large family with many people related to one another.

By the time the procession reached the wooden church, the crowd had grown. There was already a group of people outside the church waiting for the family to arrive. The coffin was inside and open, as it was the tradition to view the deceased during the church service. After everyone sat down, the priest signalled the congregation to arise. The choir lead the congregation in some old favourite home-going songs. The sound of singing and weeping blended together like soprano and alto, complementing one another. Bee still did not show any real emotions. The procession left the church for the short walk back to the small cemetery on the hill. Bee and her siblings were given chairs to sit on while the priest presided over the last moments and songs before their mother was laid to rest. Everyone was wrapped up in his or her own grief, so much so that no one noticed Bee's blank expression. The four coffin bearers lowered the coffin into the grave. The priest sprinkled his handful of earth on the coffin. From dust you came and unto dust you will return. That was when everyone heard the scream, as the volcano in Bee's heart erupted. One of the coffin bearers grabbed hold of Bee's hand just as she was about to fall on the coffin. Others rushed in to help. The coffin leaned to one side as Bee began to scream 'Mummy, mummy! Don't leave me Mummy. Come back!' She was like a someone possessed. She kicked and punched anything that came close. It took four grown men to hold her down while she screamed for her mother. Bee's heart drummed in her chest like an African drum as she bawled down the cemetery.

2

A few hours later, Bee woke up in a strange room feeling thirsty, as if she had been running a marathon. Three elderly ladies sat around her bed, wiping her face with a damp cloth and saying their rosaries. 'Chile we thought we had lost you! But God is good! He answered our prayers!'

That was when Bee realised it was not a dream. God did not answer her prayers. Bewildered, Bee wept into her pillow. Then softly she started to recite the prayer they said every night before bed. *This night as I lay down to sleep, I pray the Lord my soul to keep. If I should die before I wake, I pray the Lord my soul to take. In my little bed I lie, heavenly father hear my cry. Lord, protect me through this night and bring me safe til morning light.* One of the women gave her a handkerchief. AMEN. God will take care of you chile. Bee lay back into the little bed staring at the ceiling as if the answer to her prayer was hidden somewhere up there. Slowly she fell asleep. And this is how Bee started life without a mother.

Chapter One

By the time Bee was ten years old, she had already lost both her parents. Since that time she had been brought up by her older brother and older sister, in the village of La Femme, in St David's. Like most children, Bee had to help around the house before and after school, as well as help her brother and sister. They were labourers in the harvesting season, planting and growing anything that they could sell in the local market. It was the 1960s. Life was hard and there were no laws protecting children from hard labour in Grenada.

Bee found life very tiring. The only free time she had was on a Sunday when she went to church and sang in the choir. She had a beautiful, soulful voice which lifted the whole congregation. It was one of those Sundays which changed the course of Bee's life.

On that special Sunday, the church was packed to welcome the new missionary, David, his wife Florence, and their twelve and thirteen year old sons, Matthew and Mark. The vicar delivered a special service to introduce the new missionary. Sunday service was a grand event for most villagers. Having worked all week, Sunday was when they got to dress up in their best clothes and congregate with everyone to praise the Lord in song and prayer. That Sunday, Bee was asked to sing a solo.

Bee chose the song her mother used to sing while she cooked and washed in the river. Bee had heard this song everyday and used to sing along with her mother; the words had become engraved in her heart.

When the moment came for Bee to sing, she stood up in front of the congregation. She was a shy girl, but it was as if her mother was with her that day. She felt as if she w watching her from Heaven. Bee closed her eyes then belted out *The Old Rugged Cross*. Her singing stroked the hearts of even the hardest of men in the congregation and lifted the spirits of everyone present. Her singing brought hope. There was not a dry eye in the church when Bee finished her solo. The small wooden church resounded and reverberated with *Amen, Praise the Lord, Hallelujah*. Bee's voice also captivated the new missionary, who felt he had witnessed something special.

After the service, the missionary and his family were invited to the vicar's house for dinner. The vicar and his wife lived in the old plantation house near to the church. The house had four bedrooms, a big kitchen and living room, with nice old furniture. The yard was planted with crotons in beautiful deep reds, yellows and greens, with red hibiscus along the front. They had no children. They had a helper for the yard and to clean the house, but the vicar's wife did all the cooking.

As they sat around the dining table overlooking the garden, the missionary could not get Bee's voice out of his mind.

"Who is this girl who sang this morning?" he asked the vicar.

And so the vicar told the missionary Bee's story. How Bee's father had died suddenly and nobody knew what was wrong with him. He was a healthy, hard working man, who, one morning just didn't wake up. Then Bee's mother contracted pneumonia, which she never recovered from. She died, leaving six children behind. Bee was just ten years old.

The missionary and his family lived in an old great house which was in need of a lot of upkeeping. They had hired a few helpers around the house, however they were not satisfied with their work ethics. The missionary could not get accustomed to how laid back the locals were, interpreting this custom as laziness and unreliability.

Florence, the missionary's wife, was a strong and hard-working. She was a big woman, with a pretty face, brown hair and strong arms. She was accustomed to home keeping, and so she did most of the house work herself. Nonetheless, it was too much for her to do.

We cannot go on like this David. We have to do something! Florence said to her husband, as they lay in bed one night reading. David had his Bible open, his glasses on the tip of his nose, making notes in an old leather-jacket journal. Florence was reading her tattered copy of Charlotte Bronte's *Jane Eyre*. She had read it so many times, the pages were brown and fragile, but each time it brought new meaning to her and the same romantic tears to her green eyes.

The next morning at the breakfast table, the missionary told Florence what he had in mind.

I have an idea that will kill two birds with one stone."

What does the Bible say about killing David dear? Florence asked him.

No, I am serious, David replied.

Well then! I am all ears.

"What about if we take in Bee to live with us full time?"

Florence's eyes widened with surprise. "How will that work?"

"Well," said David, "she can come and live with us and help you with the housework. She won't have to work so hard in the fields anymore and we can help her get a good education. And she would be good company for you as well. Think about it. The boys will be leaving home before you know it. Making their way into the world."

Florence turned it over in her head, trying to suppress her great delight in her husband's proposal. She wasn't sure about the idea. She didn't want to take a ten year old child as a servant. And although she had always wanted a daughter, this was not the same. She always felt the boys were old enough to help around the house, but their father insisted they spent all their time with their books. When Florence was growing up, her brothers helped out in the farm which her parents ran, while she and her sister had to help their mother with all the house work. Everybody did something and that is how she learned to be such a great housekeeper, wife and mother.

And so it was; Bee moved in with the missionary and his family. In those days, it was common for people to take children from large families or those struggling. These children would help with the work around their homes, but very often they were mistreated by their guardians. However Bee had no say in the matter. All she knew was that her sister had packed her school uniform, her two church dresses and her one pair of church shoes, in the small grip which had been her mother's. She was told that she was going to live with the white people from the church. Just like that.

"Them is good people. Just behave yourself. Work hard and study you school work like a good girl," her sister told her. "You don't know how lucky you is! You know how much girls wish they could be in your shoes? Ah wish was me!"

Bee's sister Bernadette was nineteen years old. All she did was work hard to feed her younger brothers and sisters and to send them to school. All she knew was how to survive.

Florence didn't want it to appear as if Bee was their servant, she wanted Bee to feel like part of the family. So she prepared the small room in the loft for Bee.

It was the first time Bee had a room to herself. She was used to sleeping on the floor in their little house, with her sister next to her and her brother on the bench. The room Florence prepared had a small narrow bed in one corner, with a small lamp on a little table beside it and an old rocking chair with one arm broken where she put her little grip. There was a small window overlooking the vegetable garden behind the house.

When the Missionary told their sons about the arrangement, Matthew and Mark found it strange to suddenly have a local girl from the village in their home, living as part of their family. It took them a while to get accustomed to it. They were, however, delighted to have someone else to play tricks on, using their likeness to get away with pranks.

Chapter Two

If Bee hadn't stayed in that bathroom longer than usual that morning, and Florence had not gone up to her room to check on her, she would not have known something was wrong.

Florence did notice that Bee had gained a bit of weight, even though lately she seemed to have lost her hearty appetite, picking at her food. Normally Bee devoured her meals, marvelling at the abundance of food that was always available. She also ate whatever the boys did not want, yet still she was always hungry. Bee thought about her own home and how they never had enough. Her older brother and sister worked so hard and struggled to make ends meet. Her sister had to stretch everything to feed all of them. Bee loved fruits, but no amount of mangoes, golden apples or plums could quell that pang of hunger which was always there, niggling at her stomach.

"Bee are you okay?" Florence called as she went upstairs to check on Bee.

Bee had gone back to bed, feeling too weak to go back downstairs after vomiting everything she had in her stomach. She had been feeling ill in the mornings and had started spitting a lot, something she herself could not stand to see people doing. She didn't feel like getting up and felt too weak to do her morning chores. However, by mid morning she was usually back to her old self, singing away while she swept the yard and fed the chickens, her sweet voice floating into the house.

"My dear child! You look terrible." Florence said, bending to feel Bee's forehead. Bee groaned and curled up on the bed, holding her tummy.

"Ah feeling sick Miss Florence."

Huge waves of sickness washed over her. Her legs felt too weak to walk down the stairs.

Bee groaned and curled up tighter as another wave of nausea hit her. Her head spun. The room too. "I must take you to the doctor Bee. How long have you been feeling sick?" Florence asked, worry creasing her brows. But Bee could not remember when her food started refusing to stay in her stomach.

Dr Joseph showed up early a few days after Florence had taken Bee to see him. They were having breakfast. That morning Florence had made pancakes. Bee loved pancakes. Her sister made bakes and dumplings with flour, making enough to feed them all. But she loved this new thing Ms Florence made with the same flour. And it was the only thing that did not make her feel sick these days.

"Oh, what a pleasant surprise to see you Dr Joseph." Florence said, as she ushered him into the living room. "Can I offer you a cup of tea, Doctor?"

"Oh, a pleasant morning Florence. Thank you, but I cannot stay."

By now the boys were ready for school so Florence saw them off. The school was only half a mile away.

"Where is David?" the doctor asked.

"He is in the back garden. I will get him."

"So how is Bee these days? Still in bed?"

"Well she doesn't seem to be getting better but she is now eating like a horse! Must be making up for when she

10

couldn't eat!" Florence smiled. "Have you found out what kind of virus it is Doctor?"

"I think I know what's wrong. I had better wait for your husband to come." As he spoke those words, David walked through the door.

"Good morning David." Dr Joseph said with a serious voice.

"Pleasant morning Doctor. You have some news for us I take it?" David asked.

"You two had better sit down."

David and Florence sat on the old mahogany sofa. The brown upholstery was faded and threadbare in some places, the arm rest well worn. David reached over and held Florence's hand, a gesture performed out of habit, for comfort.

Bee had been living with the family for two years and she had shown herself to be a great help to Florence. Bee was hard working and she had learned quickly. Florence was teaching her to sew and helping her to read. And Bee kept the house cleaner than it had ever been. Nothing was too much for Bee to do. And although Florence didn't want Bee to have to do so much, whilst wishing the boys would help out more, she felt they had made the right decision taking Bee to live with them.

"Well Doctor?" David said, his voice stiff with tension.

"Well we have the test results back," the doctor said. When Florence had taken Bee to him, she had told Dr Joseph a bit about Bee's history and how had come to live with them.

"I don't know how to say this, but I think the girl is pregnant." Dr Joseph said. Although Florence has been careful to emphasize that Bee was considered as part of their family, the daughter she never had, Dr Joseph could not bring himself to say "your daughter".

Florence's intake of breath punctuated the silence. David squeezed her hand. His grip firm and strong, summoning her composure.

"I think the girl is over two months pregnant. Do you know if anyone has interfered with her?"

"Oh God no!" Florence's hand flew to her mouth. "No! How can this be? She is only 12 years old! David? How could this be? She is just a little girl!" Florence stood up. Walked to the window. The room was quiet. She stood there looking out of the window into the garden, as if the answers were somewhere out there.

"Has the girl seen her period yet?" the doctor asked.

"Florence?" David queried, eyebrows arched, looking at his wife. These personal matters he left to his wife. This was embarrassing him. Not to mention the shame. He was a man of God. The disgrace. The sin! Right under his roof.

"Um, no! Oh, I don't know. I don't think so." Florence said. And she realized that she had never discussed these matters with Bee. Her own mother had never explained them to her nor her sisters. When she was fourteen she saw blood on her knickers for the first time, it didn't scare her that much. She knew what to do because she had seen her older sister using cloths and washing them every month. She just thought that she would know, that Bee would come to her when it happened to her. Well, she didn't think about it really. Bee was only twelve years old, still just a young girl. But she had heard of cases where girls got pregnant as early as ten years old.

After Dr. Joseph had left the house, Florence and David sat in silence. Neither said a word for what seemed like eternity. Florence did not know what to do. She did not know where to let her thoughts wander or her mind linger.

She had noticed how quickly Bee was maturing, how her breasts seem to be swelling under her dresses, which were already too tight. But Bee had a good appetite, so Florence didn't make too much of it. And she knew that Bee didn't really have contact with any men, apart from her older brother whom she rarely saw.

Florence was tormented by thoughts and so many questions. For two nights she lay in her bed wide awake, pondering on their situation. Everything seemed to have slowed down or come to a halt. Florence couldn't look at Bee without getting a lump in her throat. Bee's appetite was back and she was more her old self, but Florence could see the child had no clue what was happening to her. There was no way Bee could have had contact with a man. So how did this happen? When could this have happened?

These questions would linger in her mind for some time to come. Meantime, Florence knew she had to focus on the present. She had to steer her family forward through the shockwaves caused by the situation. She knew it could only be a matter of time before she would have to sit down with David and her sons to discuss the new reality.

Matthew and Mark were still at school. Bee had come home early. Florence could not wait any longer. They had to talk to Bee and do something about this situation.

Florence tried to compose herself and calm the torrent of emotion overwhelming her. She and David were in the same seats as when Dr Joseph had given them the news. Bee sat on the single armchair across from them.

Since Florence had told her they needed to talk to her, Bee felt even sicker with worry, wondering what she had done wrong. She did all her house work just as Miss Florence asked her to do. She never complained. She especially liked cleaning the main house, wandering into all the rooms, singing softly while she brushed the cob webs, swept up the dust hiding in the corners below the chairs and behind doors, dusted the old furniture, which smelled damp and musty. She liked lingering in the living room, with all the ornaments which she carefully cleaned and replaced. Her voice floated in and out of rooms like the spirits which she was sure filled the old house.

"Bee we need to talk to you. Remember our visit to Dr Joseph when you were very ill? Well he came to see us today with your results of your test."

Bee was worried she had done something to make her step mother and father angry. But what did it have to do with the doctor?

"Bee you know we are a family and we will stand by you. All that we ask is that you will tell us the truth. You know that the bible says you must tell the truth and the truth shall set you free. And no matter what, this will always be your home. "

Florence now had her hands clasped in her lap, as if she was praying for the right words.

"Dr Joseph thinks you are over two months pregnant. Tell me child, who has done this to you? What is his name? Where does he live?"

Bee's eyes drifted to the floor. She studied the slots between the old wood flooring, crammed with dust. She must remember to get the broom between them next time. Florence's words wafted straight past her.

Bee knew that something was happening to her, but she didn't have a clue what Florence meant by the word 'pregnant'. It started that night when that thing happened. She thought it was a dream. Every night in her sleep, the dream came back to her. Every night she felt as if something tied her to the bed. It covered her mouth with one hand. It stole her voice. Almost stifled her. It warned her not to tell anybody about what happened. And when Bee jumped up from the dream, it was just as if she could still smell that scent. The stale sweat and garlic smell. It always stayed in the room.

"What is pregnant?" Bee asked.

"Well," Florence said, choosing her words carefully, "that is what happens when you are going to have a baby."

Before Bee could digest this David stepped in.

"Do you have a boyfriend Bee?" he asked, sternly.

"No!" Bee sharply replied. Florence swiftly intervened, not giving Bee time to digest all this.

"Bee, to get pregnant you must be with someone." She calmly said. " You must be with a man. Bee, you must tell us who did this to you. Think back around two months ago".

Confusion and dread bathed Bee. Nobody ever told her about being pregnant or having a baby. She had seen lots of women with big bellies. She had heard people talking about it and seen them with babies, but she had never even heard the word pregnant. Miss Florence said you have to be with a man for this thing to happen. Images from that night flashed in her mind. "Tell us child. Don't be afraid. Everything will be okay. Just tell us the truth. Remember, tell the truth always."

Bee was a truthful girl. She could only tell the truth but this meant remembering what she thought was a dream and telling Florence the truth.

It was a warm night and Bee was in bed without the cover. The small kerosene lamp was lighting low, not enough to lighten the room. Suddenly, Bee woke up as she felt something on her legs. She could not move. She was paralyzed with fear and confusion. Since she had moved into that room in the loft, she had been having bad dreams. She was not used to sleeping in a room by herself. Her room was also all the way at the top of the house, so she had been afraid at night time. She didn't know if she was dreaming or not. Somebody was holding her down to the bed so she could not move. Her mouth kept opening but she could not say a word, as if the thing had taken her voice too. But she was not dreaming. She could feel something wet dripping onto her face. And something was parting her legs. Breathing heavy. She knew she was awake, but still she was not sure. She tried to call out, but it was like, in her dream, no sound came out. Something was pressing inside her. It was hurting her. A white hot pain, as if a flash of lightening had just ripped something between her legs. Then the thing was gone.

Bee wanted to get up, but her legs would not move. So she just lay there in the dark silence, drenched in the thing's sweat, her legs spread open with something wet between them. And that smell. The smell stayed behind, in the room, with her. Then it came back again, as if it had forgotten something. Forgotten to take that smell it left behind. Bee kept her eyes shut and prayed.

She knew that smell. It sat by her on the dining table; it leaned over her to correct her spellings and made sure she pronounced her words correctly; it walked to school with her; it hugged their mother and said "Mum" in the sweetest voices; it played cricket in the road with the other boys; it walked to church and sat on either side of Miss Florence and Mr David, bibles in hand, like normal boys. *Miss Florence didn't smell so*. She bathed every night. She smelled like the roses from the garden. Bee knew because she had to bring in the water from the tank.

Sometimes Bee dreamed the same dream. She would wake up and when she fell asleep again, the dream continued. Maybe it was one of those dreams that kept coming back. But the smell stayed with her all the time. It stayed in her nostrils, so every time she breathed it nearly

16

choked her. It was a stale sweaty smell, mixed with a kind of garlic smell. And something else. A scent that was lodged somewhere in her memory.

Chapter Three

The truth shall set you free. The truth shall set you free. Those words played in Bee's head as she sat in front of her adopted parents, shaking with fright. She had now shed the load which rested on her back like a sack of wet cocoa. A load she had been carrying for months, draining her energy and making her sick. She did not understand how a dream could make her run to the toilet to vomit like that. Bee wanted that dream to go away. She wanted to get her voice back and to eat mangoes again. But Miss Florence said she was having a baby. How she could be having a baby? Her older sister didn't even have a baby yet. And Bee didn't know anything about making a baby. Bee thought her belly was getting bigger because of all the mangoes she was eating, even though she had to vomit every time they touched her stomach.

Neither Florence nor David could utter a word for what seemed like ages. The sun had not gone down yet. It's soft, warm rays spilled into the living room, but somehow it felt dark. Florence loved that time of day, those hours between the close of the afternoon and arrival of the night, signalling a time for rest and new beginnings. Each day she looked forward to this time, when the family came together for dinner, the aroma of stew and fried potatoes wafting from the kitchen, the children doing their homework and later their bible studies.

"Child what are you saying?" Florence was the first to break that uncomfortable silence which now filled the room. "Somebody came into your room! Is that what you are saying Bee? How could that have happened? Who could come into your room in the night, child? What nonsense are you talking about Bee?"

Bee lifted her head to look at Mr David and Miss Florence. Miss Florence told her that the truth was going to set her free but she didn't feel free at all. She felt as if somebody had heaved that sack of cocoa on her back again. It was wet and heavy, dripping with fright and confusion. Bee felt the urgent need to run outside and spit, but could not get up and go outside, so she swallowed. She swallowed the bitterness left in her mouth by this messy situation.

David sat in stunned silence.

"Bee I am talking to you. How could somebody come into your room?"

"I don't know Miss."

"Why didn't you tell us?" Florence was beside herself with dread.

"I don't know Miss Florence. I was afraid. I thought I was dreaming."

"You're not making this up now child, are you? Please tell the truth Bee. Remember what we always tell you."

Bee could not stop herself shaking. She did not know what to say. She was confused now. She knew it was not a dream. She knew something happened to her, but she did not understand what.

"Did you see who it was child?"

"No Miss. I was afraid Miss."

Florence looked at Bee sitting across from them. The child was trembling. Florence was lost for words. She felt a cold dread creeping up her spine as the magnitude of the

19

situation confronted her. She knew Bee did not tell lies. Bee was brought up to know the word of God. She was a good girl. Obedient. She did not have to be told what to do. She was such a great help to Florence, just like David said she would be. Florence was very pleased they had taken her into their home.

David paced the room, frustration and disbelief weighing his steps. Florence didn't know what to make of David's silence. He was the one always in charge, always knowing what to say and how to resolve problems, whether they were home or community based. Now they were hit with this right under their roof and he seemed to have lost his voice.

Dread tightened its fist around Florence's heart as she begged God to forgive the unpleasant thoughts crashing around in her head. But she was a sensible woman. She knew enough and had heard enough about situations where men turned to young girls, sometimes even their own daughters, for sexual pleasures. Her mind wandered into the bedroom which she and David shared. Ever since they moved to the island, they had slept in separate beds. The heat was her excuse. David came to her bed to fulfil his very regular urges. He climbed onto her, and a few grunts later, he collapsed onto her, breathing like someone about to have a heart failure. Often, she pretended to be asleep. Since she had given birth to Mark, Florence experienced very little pleasure from these encounters. David would return to his bed, leaving her with unfulfilled desires and that slightly repulsive body odour she had grown accustomed to. She was happy to settle for her romance novels, where she could dream her dreams.

Florence too, swallowed hard, as she tried to get rid of that nasty taste which had gathered in her mouth. She knew deep down there was no way Bee had chance to be with any man. Apart from school and church, Bee was always at home, and when they went to church she sat with them. Her fears that it was someone in their home was now real, but it was a truth she was not prepared to deal with. She wished she could bury this sordid secret with everything else that might be lurking under the floorboards of the old plantation house. She imagined the scandal it would rouse in their community if word got out. They were God fearing people and must deal with this fairly. As much as she wished she did not have to, she knew she had to confront this. They had to take action and they had to do it fast. She had to get to the bottom of this mess. *God Almighty! How will we deal with this? The shame! The scandal!* No. She vowed to herself that she would do all she could to keep her family's reputation from being tarnished. Whatever the outcome, no one will know!

Chapter Four

David contacted the leader of the Mission about the situation and prayed they could offer a solution. The few days it took for them to receive an answer dragged on painfully, and the tension grew thick and heavy in their home. They felt so alone and frustrated.

David was consumed with worry about his reputation, the family's name, bringing such dishonour to the Church. How they would look in the eyes of the community if word got out? What if they had to leave the island? Go back to England? That would be devastating! He had built a good honourable life in the community. It was their home. A home he had grown to love. A blessing.

Meanwhile, Florence was tormented by thoughts she could neither bury nor set free. The questions which she could not bring herself to ask nudged her each time she tried to push them out of her mind. They niggled her every conscious moment, shook her awake and kept her pondering through the nights. She prayed with her entire being for the merciful father to remove those ugly thoughts from her head. She searched for some kind of sign, some form of conviction in David's face, now creased with consternation, his shoulders slumped with worry. She longed to be delivered from the grips of this dread which now settled in her gut.

Florence and David spoke to Bee in her room. They had received word from England. The news lifted a weight from their shoulders, a weight which had almost sunken them beneath the floorboards. They now sat to disclose even more secrets. Secrets which would send Bee on a path which would affect generations to come.

David had already started to cover up the secret. Telling the villagers that they were sending Bee abroad for her schooling. She was such a bright child that they did not want her to waste any opportunity.

The Saturday morning was still wet from the rainfall that night and the air was damp with the smell of nutmegs and cinnamon. Normally they would be out doing the works of God, spreading his word and bringing more numbers to the church, but there were crucial matters to deal with and the sooner the better.

They all sat around the sitting room in their own silence. Matthew and Mark sat next to each other. The boys could feel something was wrong. Bee sat in the arm chair, her eyes downcast. She knew this gathering had something to do with her, but she had no idea what was coming. "Let us close our eyes and bow our heads for a moment as I pray for God's direction on this situation we have found ourselves in as a family." David broke the silence. "Oh God, we have sinned against you and one another. We ask for your forgiveness and peace and we pray you will give us a new start in Jesus' name. Amen."

Florence said a brisk Amen and left David to break it.

"Your mother and I have decided to send Bee to England. We have spoken to the church up there and they will take Bee in to finish her education. She will have the chance to make a better life for herself," David said, looking straight at his sons as he spoke, as if somehow it didn't concern Bee but had everything to do with them. Why was their father looking at them in that way? The boys looked at their father, then at each other. Neither of them could look at Bee. They kept their eyes on their hands, on the floor, anywhere except at Bee. Ever since that night they had tried their hardest to avoid her.

Bee's eyes flew, first to Florence then David. She did not understand what she was hearing. *Sending her to England? What they sending her there for?* Since Miss Florence told her about the baby, Bee had not been able to think about anything else. Every night she lay in her bed thinking about it: how she was going to make the baby; how her clothes were getting too tight; how her belly was growing. And every night she dreamed the same dream. She did not tell Miss Florence and Mr David that the thing happened twice. That, the same night, it came back again. How she had shut her eyes so tight she was afraid she wouldn't be able to open them again. How she had kept them shut tight until that smell left her alone.

"Bee, it will be a good opportunity for you. You will stay with our friends from our church. They are good people. They will care for you and you will have a good education." David continued, choosing his words carefully as his conscience pricked him. They had not told the boys anything about the situation. Florence had thought it best to disclose as little as possible. One can never be too careful.

Seeing the confusion on Bee's face, Florence intervened.

"My dear child, this is a wonderful opportunity for you! Everything is going to be fine. When we come to England we will visit you. You will be in great hands."

When Florence and David broke the news to Bee's older brother and sister, they could not have been happier for Bee. Bee was getting the chance they all dreamed about. Going abroad was a dream many had but few could fulfil. To them, England was The Mother Land, a place where streets were paved with gold and life was good. In their eyes Bee's luck had struck.

Bee sat in a daze, unable to grasp the reality of the situation, but she was beginning to get the picture. They were sending her to England. Bee knew that people were always talking about going to England and America. She knew people who had gone and sent for their children. But she did not have any family away. She liked living with Miss Florence and Mr David but she knew they were sending her away because of the bad thing that happened to her.

"Miss, I don't want to go! Please Miss. I will go back by my brother and sister." Bee sobbed uncontrollably.

"Stop it child! This is the only way God is going to forgive you for what you have done!" David said, trying to keep the guilt and shame from his voice. "The decision has been made. You will go to England. Now go to your room child."

Bee staggered up the stairs like a criminal sent to the gallows. She lay on the bed with a pillow over her head as tears shook her body. With fear and sadness she remembered feeling the same pain and grief when she had seen her mother lying in the open coffin. She did not understand it but it frightened her. Just like this situation frightened her. She wished she could go back to the way things were, before she came to live with Florence and David; swimming in the river, climbing mango trees and just playing in the street with her friends. Memories of her childhood drifted in and out as she lay there, stricken with sadness. She did not remember much of her father but a particular memory floated like a feather from the yard where she had played as a little girl. It landed right on the bed next to her: her father coming home from work, how he laughed a lot, tickling her as he dug into his pocket for the sweets he had brought home for her. And that smell on his breath. Her mother would say "leave the chile alone wid you drunk self," and push him away when he staggered near to her. That's the smell she remembered on his breath.

Maybe what happened to her was a dream. Was it a dream? She had washed away the dirtiness she felt. And every Sunday in church Bee had prayed for God to take away that thing that happened to her. To wash away the ugliness she felt inside. But the smell would not go away. It filled up her nose and lingered in her head. She would remember it for as long as she lived.

Matthew and Mark were stunned! What did Bee do? Why were their parents sending her away. They did not understand but were afraid to ask. Could it have anything to do with them? Ever since that night, they had avoided Bee as much as they could. Each of the boys had stowed far away the events of that night, too full of shame to talk about it. They both shivered, even though the mid morning glow filled the room with its warmth. The memories of that night were as potent as the spirits they had consumed that day. The memories burned their throats just like the spirits did.

Matthew and Mark were out in the woods hunting with some local boys, when they came across an illegal rum making camp that produced a 100% proof rum known as *Fire Water*. Being boys, they had dared each other to taste the spirits. One by one they had tried it, screaming and spitting as it threatened to blow their heads off. Not to be undone, the brothers had looked at each other with pure mischief in their eyes. Matthew went first, taking in a bit and spitting it out with the cry it forced from him. Then Mark, the younger of the two, psyched himself up for the challenge. He closed his eyes as he slowly brought the cup to his lips. The fumes almost choked him but he swallowed. His mouth was on fire but he swallowed. His belly was ablaze and his eyes went red. He tried to drown the pain with water but the force of the spirits escaped in the scream he let out. Mark thought he was going to die. His blood boiled but he refused to react until he could not keep the rum down any longer, vomiting everything that he had eaten that day. The boys vowed to not to tell anyone.

They went to bed early that night. Florence noticed they were extra jovial, talking more than usual and how they seem to have a lot to laugh about. But she didn't find it strange. They were very close and very lively boys. They had always been. Almost like twins. Florence had often admired twins, their uncanny similarities, and their unique connection. Although she had never really wished for twins herself, she did not mind if God had seen it fit to bless her with a pair. So when eleven months later she gave birth to her second born, Matthew, her belief in the wonderful works of God became deeper and more profound than ever. They were so close in age, they were like twins.

Still tipsy from the spirits, all kinds of thoughts played around in the brothers' minds, especially images of Bee bathing in the river that time they had seen her there. Images of Bee's naked breasts; like two ripe mangoes. Her buttocks like two breadfruits; her cocoa tea skin; her hair which was always in plaits, flowing down her back like a black waterfall. They were used to seeing Bee just like a sister: doing some kind of house work; sewing; helping to cook; sweeping the house; doing her homework This new image of Bee had captivated them. They had lost their appetite, full on lust and passion which food could not quench. They had never seen their mother and father showing affection other than holding hands when they were going to church. And they made nothing of the afternoon

27

they came home early and found their parents' room door locked. Now they understood the sermon that preachers often preach about; King David's desire for Bathsheba, who was another man's wife. Waves of adolescent desire jolted through the brothers like electricity. They were so overcome by these new feelings, they could not sleep.

"Let's play a joke on Bee. Matthew said to Mark. "I dare you to creep into her room and lie in her bed. She won't know which one of us it was."

"Why me?" I dare *you*!" Mark challenged Matthew, but they both dismissed it. Or so it seemed.

Later, one of the brothers crept across the landing and up into the loft room where Bee slept. He opened the door as quietly as he could. The hinges cried out, but it didn't wake Bee. It just blended in chorus with all the other noises which the old house was known for at nights: creaking floor boards, noisy roof, rusted hinges, together with all the other mysterious ones.

Mark crept over to Bee's bed, wearing only his night dress. As he came nearer to the bed his excitement spread like a wild fire. He knew that what he was doing was wrong but Mark could not stop himself now. His body was doing funny things and he could not control it. He was fourteen years old. He never held hands or kissed a girl. But he had read about sex between a man and a woman, although he could never imagine his parents doing it. Mark could not explain what happened once he got into the bed with Bee. It was as if all those images and sinful thoughts took possession of his body. He could not stop himself. It was over in seconds.

Chapter Five

Matthew and Mark drifted outside together, like they always did. Inseparable, playing cricket in the yard; going on adventures in the woods, exploring their little village.. They shared everything, wearing each other's clothes, staying up at nights talking about everything. But what they had done that night was a secret each of the brothers kept to himself. Each one had his own thoughts, wondering if the other one knew. And it had haunted them ever since, but neither of them had breathed a word. Until that Saturday morning.

The morning brightened up and the sun was out in full, spreading its rays over the garden. Everything was in bloom: the hibiscus was the most brilliant red it had ever been, the petals of the pale yellow roses soft and creamy like vanilla ice cream, the bougainvilleas seeming to be taking over, running radiant and wild. Yet a stifling dampness pervaded, casting its gloomy shadow over the entire household.

Florence had not moved from where she sat all morning. Somehow she could not shift the weight she felt, nor muster enough energy to get up and get on with her Saturday routine. It was not life as usual in their household. She just needed that stillness. She wanted to sit in silence with God the Almighty, the God they had dedicated their lives to, given up their native home for, to be on this island to carry out his works. Perhaps all their troubles would somehow dissipate, vanish into the silent space which surrounded her soul. Perhaps if she just sat there, without movement, without thoughts - not really possible - perhaps it would all go away and her family would be spared.

David stood by the window, engulfed in his own silence and troubled conscience. He was God's messenger, called upon to spread the gospel and serve God. He had sinned and feared what punishment he would face in the eyes of God. This whole sordid situation had made him tell lies, keep the truth hidden. He had lied to Bee's brother and sister. And at church when the doctor had enquired about Bee's situation and what the family was going to do, he had prayed for redemption as he made up a story about Bee being raped by a man from the village. He had also told the doctor of their decision, but looking at his sons, David got a niggling feeling a lot more prayers were needed.

The brothers did not know why Bee was being sent away, but they felt it had something to do with that night. Relief lightened the weight they had carried on their shoulders since that night, which was a night they each remembered with confusion and shame. With Bee leaving, they would not have to work at avoiding her anymore. They could go back to how things were before she came to live with them. But something was wrong. Why were their parents sending her for a better education in England, when their own sons were being schooled in Grenada? If that was why Bee was going away, how come their parents looked so worried?

"Do you know what's happened to Bee?" Matthew asked Mark, looking at his younger brother intently.

"I don't know? Why you asking me?" Mark's face turned a close shade of bird cherry.

"Where did you go that night Mark? I saw you! Did you go to Bee's room?"

30

Matthew waited for Mark's response, with no intention of disclosing any details of his own little secret. What happened next took both boys by surprise. Mark pushed Matthew with a force of anger that almost pelted his brother into the rose patch. The punch which Mark received in return landed directly on his nose. Mark fell to the ground like a coconut with blood pouring from his face.

David could not believe what was unfolding right before his eyes! His sons, these two boys whom he had brought up in the church to renounce all forms of violence, were fighting!

Mark's cry pulled Florence out from her state of trance. She was the first to run out the door. David followed.

"Boys! What's the matter with you?" David shouted.

"Mark! What's happened?" Florence asked, concern creasing her usually cheerful face.

"Get inside this minute! Both of you!" David said.

It was the first time they had heard their father raise his voice this way. It terrified them. They both hurried inside. Mark covered his bloody nose with his shirt.

The parents were in shock. They had never experienced violence in their family before. Florence grabbed hold of Mark, pulling him away to see to his nose.

"What are you fighting about boy?" Florence asked.

David took Matthew into the kitchen to calm down while Florence cleaned up Mark's bloody face. She had never seen that side of her precious sons before. What was happening to their family?

The disturbance woke Bee, who had fallen asleep from her crying spell and thought she was dreaming again. It was Saturday and she should be doing her chores. She wondered what the noise was but she did not know if she could go downstairs yet.

Bee wondered what it would be like in England. Maybe it would be better for her if she did go. Everybody talked about going away to England or America as if it were the best thing. Her friends envied her, wishing it were them going. Little did they know. They had no idea about Bee's situation. She was twelve years old and going to be a mother. She did not even understand how that happened to her. All she knew was that something or somebody came into her room and left a baby in her belly. And a bad smell in her nose. That smell revisited her room every night and haunted her. You see people looking normal, as if everything was alright, but you never knew what was really going on. None of them knew how frightened Bee was. How she had not been able to sleep since that night. How worried she had been since Mr David told her they were sending her away. She knew nothing about where they were sending her or with whom she was going to be staying.

Bee didn't even know that her worries and sleepless nights showed until her sister noticed the dark shadows around her eyes, when Bee went to say good bye.

"What happen to you Bee?" Her sister had asked her. "Girl you going in England! You should be happy! How come you looking miserable so? You en know how lucky you is! Ah wish was me!

Maybe she was lucky in truth. Maybe when she went away her bad dreams would go away. Maybe they would stay behind, in that little room in the loft, leave her alone.

Chapter Six

Bee's departure date came around before she had time to let the reality of the whole thing settle in her head. David hired a car to take the family to the airport. The car rolled along the village like the river flowing down past the banana, breadfruit, coconut and mango trees, which everyone in the village shared. Bee sat by the window, watching everything she had grown up with and knew as her home disappear behind the car: Ms Brown's little shop at the front of her house, where you could buy anything from flour, sugar, saltfish and rice, to needles and thread, and the best flex sweets and coconut candies you ever tasted; Mr Steadman's furniture shed, where her mother bought her dressing table one Christmas. It took her a whole year to finish paying for it with her susu money. The dressing table still stood in the corner of the bedroom which her sisters shared. The varnish was still shiny and new as new as the day her mother bought it home. The St Mary's Roman Catholic school rolled by slowly, sheep grazing on the dry, thirsty grass, instead of children playing cricket and dodge the ball. It was the Easter holiday; the village children gathered by the stand pipe, bathing, washing and filling buckets of water to carry home. They waved as the car passed them.

Bee's heart slowed down a bit, as if to take time to gather every image, pack it away and take it with her. Everybody was excited and happy about Bee's apparent fortune. She was experiencing the dream that everyone had, and wished would come true. "Make your mother proud you hear! You are a lucky child. God bless you my darling."Ms Brown said to Bee, when she went to say good bye. "Chile your mother must be smiling in she grave now. You is a lucky, lucky chile!" Miss June said, wiping tears from her gaunt cheeks as she stood on her front steps. Miss June lived next door to Bee's old home. Mavis, Miss June's crippled daughter waved from behind the closed window. People said Miss June was ashamed of her daughter, so Mavis did not go to school or church or anywhere. She was often left alone in the house while her mother went to work. She was the same age as Bee.

Florence's heart felt like lead. Her conscience had not ceased the continuous battle between her heart and her head. Questions bashed about in her head but she just pushed them to the back of her mind, afraid of the answers which might surface. The change in her sons' relationship did not go unnoticed. Matthew and Mark, once as close as their age difference, had drifted apart. At first Florence thought it was just adolescent hormones working on their individualism, but deep down she knew it was more than that. And something must have happened between the boys. Something connected with Bee. But she felt it best to leave them to work out their differences. She also noticed the shift in David's manner with the boys, which left uneasiness in her chest that grew with her questions. But some things were better left in their silence. She let sleeping dogs lie.

Florence waved until Bee stepped onto the LIAT aircraft, which would take her to Trinidad for the next flight whisking her to a new life. Florence prayed that God would take this whole situation into his hands. She did every night as she lay her troubled heart to rest.

The air hostess escorted Bee to her seat by the window and left her there. The airplane was so big. Bee wondered how this big machine could fly in the air. It was not full but there was an excitement buzzing amongst the men, women and children who had boarded the flight. Bee sat there in her own thoughts as conversations circled around her.

"So Bridgeman, you finally doin it man! It look like you hit the jackpot this time eh!"

"The jackpot is joke! England better be ready for me!"

"Margo, ah so glad for you girl. Who send for you? You uncle Ben?"

"Me uncle Ben! Girl this man never study nobody since he land in England nuh! He give all of us back. Is me mother friend that send for me, oui!"

"Aa. God is good. Children! All you mother is a good woman. God bless her. She sending for all of you! Thank you Lord! Hallelujah! Thank you Jesus! You think is easy trouble these children see! All you see this God? He is an almighty God! Praise God! All you make all you mother proud you know! Thank you Father!" Judith signed herself as she smiled at the five Campbell children, well dressed in their best clothes, going to meet their mother. She had left them with a neighbour to go away with a man who worked on the banana boat.

Bee was looking out the window when a lady sat in the empty seat next to her. The people sounded so happy. Glad they going away. They had mother, friend, sister or aunty and uncle waiting. She did not have anybody she knew. She had no idea what she was going to. Bee wished she could inhale some of the excitement. She wished she could feel a little bit of the gladness about that dream everybody dreamed and tried to plant in her heart, but her

35

reality and all her worries, fears and anxieties boarded the plane with her and sat right next to her.

"You going and meet your mother?" The lady sitting next to her asked, bringing Bee back from her thoughts.

Bee shook her head, and swallowed the tears which threatened, as sadness washed over her. She wished she was one of those children going to meet their mother. Bee kept her mother's memory alive in her sweet melodious singing. Always singing the songs she remembered singing: *The Old Rugged cross, Amazing Grace, Kumbaya Me Lord*, kumbaya while she cooked, washed and hung up clothes on the line in the yard. A gift to the young daughter who lost her mother too soon.

"Who you going to meet?" The lady asked, looking at Bee with concern. "You going by yourself?"

Bee glanced at the lady. She looked like she was in her twenties like Bee's big sister. She had a nice face, round, with a small nose, dimpled cheeks and cheerful eyes. Bee wanted to answer, but her chest was too full. She was afraid it would burst open, and her emotions would choke her if she only opened her mouth.

"Don't worry child. You go be alright. You going in England! Everything in England nice. You lucky to get the chance so young you know," the lady said to Bee. She wondered what the girl's story was. She was eleven years old, around the girl's age, when her own mother had left her with an aunt and gone to England sixteen years ago. She had not seen her mother since, nor heard much from her. It had taken her mother's death to get her on an airplane, to see her buried and meet and take care of the two younger brothers and the sister her mother left behind.

When the plane took off, excited cheers went up. Clapping. Praying. Thanking God. Bee grabbed hold of the lady's hand, trembling with fright.

"Rest your head on me shoulder child." She too was terrified by the taking off, that noise and the strangeness of being in this big machine that can float in the air. She had her own worries about her situation, but she felt something for this girl with the dark, puffy eyes, her two big plaits under her hat.

Bee had rested her head on the lady's shoulder and slept all the way to Trinidad.

"Wake up child," the lady said, shaking Bee. "We in Trinidad. We have to get out here and wait for the next plane."

"Come child, come with me. ." The lady took her hand. Bee followed, relieved she had found someone to keep company because she was so afraid. She wouldn't have know what to do. The flight left Trinidad full of passengers, who looked happy to be leaving their homeland for the mother country England.

The air hostess served dinner, plain rice with curried chicken. The smell of the food stirred her belly, warning her. But Bee was so hungry, she wolfed down her dinner, not caring about the consequences. She was not surprised when her tummy started growling for the toilet, but the plane was moving and Bee was afraid to even get up. She had this strange feeling as if the plane would fall under her, so she sat there fighting to keep down the nausea rising up past her chest, into her throat. Sweat poured down her face and she could not contain the groan which escaped her.

"You alright child? You sweating! You feeling sick?" The lady asked Bee.

Bee swallowed the mouthful of sour saliva before she could talk.

"Ah feeling to vomit," Bee said, swallowing another mouthful of spit.

Lucky for Bee the air hostess was nearby. She fetched a paper bag from the seat pocket and gave it to Bee just in time to catch all the curry and rice pouring out. Her stomach growled even more after the emptying, but Bee felt too sick to eat anything. She drank the warm cinnamon tea that the lady poured from a flask for her and took refuge in the comfort of her shoulder once again.

Bee fell into a deep, long sleep. It was as if Bee's body had shut down; as if all those nights she was unable to sleep, all those nights when she lay wide awake thinking and pondering on her situation. *Who came in her room? How she was going to make the baby?* She lay awake thinking about all the things that nobody bothered to explain to her. And it was as if everything just ganged up on her and knocked her out, putting her in a kind of a coma.

Bee used to lie awake in her little bed, in her small room, far away from the rest of the household, afraid to close her eyes. She liked having a whole room to herself but she did not like sleeping by herself. At nights, when darkness fell, all the night noises came alive. The house came alive as if manicous were walking on the roof. The floor boards creaked as if spirits were roaming the rooms. The partitions cracked like old arthritic joints. All the outside noises sneaked into her room, the frogs and crickets and all those mysterious insects joining in chorus. Bee used to like to listen to the night noises when she was in her old home, but they had taken on a different tone. Now they jeered at her, like school children teasing one another in the school yard. At night she lay awake wondering about the baby growing inside her; how was it going to come out of her? How was she going to look after it? Bee wished she was back in her old home sleeping on the floor with her sisters; all four of them jammed up in the one small room. She was safe there. Safe with what she was used to, what she knew.

38

"Get up child. We reach." The lady shook Bee, trying to smile through her own surfacing anxiety.

Ten hours later, Bee stood at Heathrow Airport feeling totally lost. The nice lady whose shoulder she had slept on helped her through customs and to get her one suitcase before they walked into the arrival lounge together. The lady's uncle was there waiting for her and she had to go.

"Just wait right here," the lady told Bee, putting her to stand with her suitcase in an open area where she could be seen easily. "Don't go anywhere you know! Stay right there. They will see you."

Florence and David told her that two nuns would meet her at the airport. She stood where the lady told her to, her small case standing beside her and her eyes making beast for two women who looked like nuns.

The airport was so busy. Bee had never seen so many lights and colours and white people in all her life. They reminded her of ants. She used to watch them going about their business, climbing up trees, foraging and carrying food in trails of what seemed like thousands, each one doing its part. And they always looked as if they were stopping to talk to one another, pass on messages.

Bee scanned the airport for some sign of the nuns, wishing she were one of those being picked up, with hugs, smiles and tears sharing all over the place. People lifting suitcases and leaving with carrying off who they came to meet. Some held up plaque cards with names on them. Bee wished she had one too, with her name, so the nuns would not miss her.

A man in a uniform walked up to Bee. The young girl in the over sized coat and wrong shoes, standing next to an old brown suitcase, had caught his attention. He had been a customs officer, working on the airport for ten years, and was used to this scene: children and adults alike, dressed in the wrong clothes for the blistering British weather, shivering like mad, with small island anxiety written all over them. Miss Florence had given her one of her old coats which was way too big for Bee, but thank God it was warm. Even so, the early April chill was eager to welcome her to the motherland, with a cold embrace.

"My dear you look lost," the man asked Bee "Is someone meeting you?"

Bee nodded. If she had not lived with the missionary family for over two years, she would not have been able to understand a thing he was saying.

"Two nuns picking me up. But I not seeing them." Bee looked around again but could see no sign of any nuns. She was starting to get worried. Her voice quivered and her tears were not far away.

"Two nuns?" the man asked, curiosity wrinkling the brows on his round, friendly face. Wondering why this child was being picked up by nuns."What's your name my dear?"

"Bee sir," Bee answered.

"Bee? Is that short for something?"

"No sir. Bee is my name. B double e.

"Wait here, I think I see them," he said to Bee, walking towards the two women covered from head to toe in black, with red faces peeping out from under their habits.

"Excuse me," he said, "Are you looking for a young girl called Bee travelling from Grenada?"

"Oh yes, yes. Where is she?" One of them said.

"But she is not supposed to be a little girl. We are expecting a young lady," the other one said. "Is that her?" she asked pointing to Bee.

"Yes, this is her," the officer answered and escorted them to Bee. "I will leave you now my dear. Take care now."

As he walked away, he could not help noticing the look of surprise on the nuns' faces. He wondered what this child's story was, but he had done his bit. He had seen so many children coming from the West Indies, some happy but many of them looking lost and frightened like deer caught in the middle of the traffic, not knowing whether to turn left or right. He wondered why these people were leaving their homes in droves to come to England. He could never understand it. But then, what did he know? Only that they were damn hard workers and minded their business and great fun.

Chapter Seven

O n a cold April morning in 1964, Bee began her new life in England, sitting in a car with these strangers: two nuns and a taxi driver. They travelled for what seemed like hours before the taxi driver said "This is London," in an accent Bee almost could not understand. As they drove through the streets of this strange land, Bee sat snuggled in her oversized coat, marvelling at the sights outside. She had never seen so many cars in her life! And the roads were so wide, not like the little narrow roads back home. The buildings were so big and so tall; they seem to reach the skies, like in the bible story about the Tower of Babel. But she could not see the sky! And the people were all covered from head to toes in the same dark colour coats, not at all like all the sunny colours back home, where you could see people's arms and legs, where men walked around bare backed and a lot of times, bare feet too.

A thick darkness hovered over the road, following them all the way from the airport. And as they passed through the city and approached East London, the streets began to get smaller, the lights faded, the sounds changed and it seemed to get colder with the darkness. Factories populated the area and there were fewer cars. It looked as though the sun was setting, but it was the smog coming from the chimneys. Even the faces of the people seemed to change. The sadness, and heaviness that rested upon Bee's heart, sank her deeper into the seat. It felt like a dream, as if she had been in a time machine. One day she was just a girl in Grenada, and the next thing she was heading to East Hardley, and a future she could hardly look forward to with any sense of optimism.

Not a word was spoken between Bee and the two nuns throughout the entire journey. Bee grew up in a culture where children did not ask questions, so she kept her mouth shut and her eyes on the window most of the times. She did not, however, miss the curious glances they cast her way nor the questions brewing behind their thick glasses.

They finally pulled outside a big gate leading to a big house. It looked like a castle in one of the books Miss Florence had about England on the bookshelf in the living room. Bee used to like to look through those thick, heavy volumes, especially the ones with pictures of kings and queens and ladies dressed in fancy gowns – made from enough material to make about six dresses instead of trailing on the floor - pinching porcelain teacups with tiny gloved hands.

Even the gate looked like a prison gate. It felt as if Bee had died and awoken in that valley of the shadow of death she often read about in her favourite Psalm 23. A cloud of loneliness overshadowed her.

As the car pulled inside they were greeted by a serious, giant of a nun, with a big mole on her chin, and a deep husky voice to match her size.

"Is this her?" She asked, looking at Bee as if she were some kind of strange creature fallen from the sky.

"We better go inside Sister," one of the nuns in the car said, in a very quiet voice, as if she was afraid she would be chastised for speaking.

When they got inside the big nun bellowed, "Take her to her room Sister Marie. Settle her in and we shall discuss this in the morning."

"Come child," Sister Marie, the nun with the kind eyes, said to Bee. She lifted the case and Bee followed her to a small room, which seem to be the basement underneath the building. There was a single bed in one corner, a small chest of drawers in the other and a tiny window with iron bars.

"This will be your room. You can put your things in the chest of drawers over there. Have a little rest. You must be tired from the flight. I will come to fetch you for supper."

With that, Sister Marie shut the door and left, cutting out the bit of light which had sneaked in when she entered the room with her. The room was like a prison cell and Bee felt as if she was in exile, cast away down below the ground, as if she was something they needed to hide away!

Bee sat on the little squeaky bed and broke down. She could not hold back the tears which had been gathering from the time the plane landed and she took her first cold breath of this grey place, England. She opened the old brown suitcase and unpacked the few items she had brought with her: three dresses, three pairs of socks, three vests, the small bible which Miss Florence had given her, the extra pair of ring combs from the pack of four and the gold comb her sister had given her with the silver sparkle dust. And as she held the comb between her fingers, memories of her mother seeped into her chest: her mother sitting on the front steps of their little house, Bee between her knees, the warm scent of petroleum jelly and coconut oil floating in and out of her nose, comforting her; her mother's melodious singing, Bee singing along until the sweet lullaby, that soon soothed her into a deep slumber on her mother's knee. Bee's sister had combed her hair with it one last time before she left Grenada, sitting on their front steps just like with her mother. She had plaited Bee's hair in corn rows: three layers, the first row resting on her neck, the other two covering them. Her sister was not blessed with their mother's beautiful voice, but they had hummed their mother's favourite song, *Amazing Grace*, in simple harmony. Bernadette's scent was milder, fresher, like a waft of coconut scented breeze.

Bee wished she was like those children on the plane with her mother somewhere waiting for her. But her mother was dead. She did not have anybody. She was all alone in a strange country. Bee had even forgotten about the baby growing inside her until she felt the jolt of hunger which rumbled her stomach. By the time the nun returned to fetch her for supper, she had cried herself to sleep.

First thing the next morning Sister Bernard, the Mother Superior, called the sisters into her office. One look at Bee and she knew they could not keep her at St Mary's Convent. Most of the girls there came highly recommended by the priest, from very reputable families who paid highly to hide away their disgraced daughters. In many of the cases these girls were disgraced by their own flesh and blood, a brother, a cousin or even their own fathers! They took on the most sensitive cases, which came at a very high price. Sister Bernard knew that the Convent's reputation was at stake. What would these parents think? Not that she was racist or anything. Did the Bible not say that God created all in His own image and likeness? God created black people too. But the situation was not explained to her properly. All she was told was to collect a young lady who was pregnant, to look after her and integrate her into the system. She had no idea the girl would be so young. And it was not that the girl's colour ever crossed her mind, but she had a job to do and the reputation of the convent was paramount. She had to guard it with all her prudence and the shrewdness she had to employ, which made her appear mean.

"Sisters, I am sorry, but we cannot keep this girl," Sister Bernard said, looking at the sisters over her glasses. "I didn't realize the girl was so young. I am also very concerned about what it would mean for the Convent. We have never had a coloured girl here before. What will our clients think? We have to think about the Convent's name.

"But where will she go Sister? The child has no one." Sister Marie felt a spot of tenderness for this lost child whom, she was sure, through no fault of hers, had ended up in this predicament. The other nun remained silent, her eyes downcast, as if afraid to even look at the Mother Superior, much less utter a word.

"I think the best place for her would be in a Home for Mother and Child. I will make some calls, see what's available. In the meantime, please keep her in her room. Sister Marie, please see to her needs but keep her out of sight. Is that understood?" The command in Sister Bernad's voice was clear.

"Yes Sister." They both answered in unison.

And so the little room in the basement became Bee's home for the next two weeks. The only times she ventured beyond the door, which shut her away from everything and everyone, was to use the discoloured toilet and the small, dented, facebasin, where she had to wash up. The room was damp, cold and musty.

Sister Marie did as she was told. She brought Bee some toiletries, as well as a face towel, a face cloth, and a few books to keep her occupied. She took Bee's meals to the room and made sure the girl was warm enough. Yet each time she shut the door behind her, she was gripped by a terrible sense of guilt. The poor child had been quarantined as if she had some kind of disease. She felt sure God was going to punish her for her part in this, but her first duty was to her superiors and to the church. Every night when she kneeled to pray she asked God to please forgive her.

Chapter Eight

Bee's next car ride, which took her to the St Augustine's Hostel, was very different from the first one. This time outside was not grey at all. The sun was out and smiling at Bee through the window, offering some reassurance. It shone so brightly it fooled her into thinking it was warm, until she got outside. Her teacher, Mr Frank, told them that there was only one Sun. That the same Sun that shone in Grenada was the same Sun in America, Canada, England, everywhere. So Bee could not understand how come the same Sun, that scorched her skin and drenched her clothes in sweat back home, threatened to freeze her like ice in England!

The St Augustine's Hostel housed juveniles who had dropped out of school, committed crimes, as well as teenage girls who were pregnant, homeless or rejected by their families.

Bee's life was placed into the hands of people she did not know, who made all the decisions for her. She was a child, after all and had no say. But she was among other girls her age, especially other black girls, who were in a similar situation to her. And so for the first time since she left her homeland Grenada, Bee felt hopeful.

The matron showed Bee around the complex, explaining the rules as she went along. "Here at St Augustine's we believe that it is important to have rules and boundaries and we expect all the girls here to co-operate.

All girls are treated equally and are expected to get involved in the day to day running and upkeep of the hostel." The room where Bee was greeted was the communal room, where they all had meals and gathered for classes. Bee liked school and was pleased to know there was a school system within the complex for the girls to carry on with their education.

The kitchen was a long space with rows and rows of cupboards, with the biggest pots Bee had ever seen anywhere.

"We have four cooks, and girls take turn to help with the cooking and all the washing up. It's all part of learning. Everything the girls do here is a part of teaching life skills, which will prepare you for independent living." Bee wondered how they washed all those giant pots and wares in the small cracked up sink she had seen in the kitchen.

The bathrooms were near to the laundry room, with a row of what looked like stalls, with showers on one side and toilets on the other.

"Each girl is responsible for doing her own laundry and all girls share in the cleaning of the bathrooms, which must be done every morning before breakfast."

Matron looked straight at Bee as she spoke. Matron, as everyone called her, was very nearly the opposite of the Mother Superior. She was a small woman with flat chest, big feet for a woman, and brown hair tied back in a bun. And her voice, although not rough, commanded obedience and respect.

The back door opened onto a huge garden that had a pond which even had fishes in it.

"In the summer the garden is a lovely place for recreation. We all take part in cleaning and planting flowers."

Bee followed Matron, taking in everything in silence. Matron pointed them out to her, as if Bee were a visitor and had a say in whether she wanted to stay or not . Not only did she not have any say, she also had no idea what it would be like or what to expect.

"Lights must be out by ten. There's to be no excessively loud talking. No shouting at each other. Girls must be seen and not heard! These are very strict rules and we expect girls to adhere to them." Bee had no problems there. She had always been an obedient girl and she was used to working. Miss Florence had taught her a lot about house-keeping so that was the least of her worries.

Bee had to share a room with another pregnant girl called Edith. Edith was a big girl. She was big all round, including a big mouth, which she used to her advantage. Even when it got her in trouble.

That evening at dinnertime Matron introduced Bee. They were all gathered around the tables in the communal room having shepherd's pie and baked beans. It was one of Bee's favourite meals. She had watched Miss Florence making it several times and she was sure she could make it by herself. Bee wondered what was so funny when some of the girls looked at her way; some laughing, others snickering, looking at Bee as if she was so different from them. *What were they laughing at? Her clothes?*

Most of the girls were wearing slacks and jumpers in various degrees of black and grey, what seemed to be the uniform shades of England. Bee's yellow cotton dress with the red cherries and apples, which she had chosen that morning, clung to her ripening, pregnant body and brightened the room. It was not warm enough for English climes, not even for what would be considered mellow spring weather. Bee was still cold, even though she had on the thick cream cardigan with heart shaped buttons, which Miss Florence had given her, as well as two pairs of black tights. Bee tried to ignore the girls and the grumblings in her stomach made it easy. She was starving!

The room which Bee had to share with Edith was just big enough to fit the two twin sized beds, one on either side of the room. There was a wardrobe at the foot of the beds which they had to share between them, and a small chest of drawers at the head of the beds. Each girl claimed the side nearest to her. There was just enough space between the beds to get through one at a time.

Bee unpacked her case once again. She did not need much space. She quite liked the cosiness of the room, especially having someone to share it with. She never liked sleeping alone. When she was alone her nightmare returned, sneaking into her room, haunting her sleep so she woke up drenched with fright and choking on that lingering scent which stayed with her until daybreak released her. It had not visited her at the convent. Perhaps it had stayed behind in that little room, up in the loft. She prayed that it would stay there, that it would not find its way to St Augustine's Hostel. *Please God.*

Chapter Nine

B ee fitted right in, despite having to come to terms with so much change in her life all at once. She was learning the ropes at St Augustine. She took her responsibilities seriously and carried out her tasks with pride and diligence, as she did with her education. She never had to be told to do anything twice. In fact, she did much more than her share, chipping in whenever necessary, helping some of the residents who found it difficult to cope with looking after their babies plus their chores. Bee even undertook neglected tasks, whether they were due to insubordination or laziness, on the part of some of the other residents.

Bee was so busy adjusting to her new life, that she often forgot she was pregnant. As spring cheered up this cold, grey, wetness with bright, colourful blossoms, her body grew and bloomed with it. By summer, Bee's body had doubled in size; her breasts threatened to burst loose from her tops; her hair grew past her shoulders, down to the middle of her back. And the baby was pushing and stretching her skin, as well as her appetite, beyond boundaries. She could not get enough to eat. On those rare summer days when it was actually warm enough to wear summer clothes and chance a few hours out in the garden, Bee noticed those changes. She had more suitable clothes to wear by then. Matron had helped her to select some from a huge box in the storeroom, a collection from various donors.

Bee settled into her routine well. She was eager to learn and took all her classes seriously. She and her roommate Edith became good friends. They stayed awake at night chatting and singing songs played on the radio. Bee sang the songs she learned in church which Edith didn't know. Edith talked a lot about herself. Her mother was born in Jamaica and taken up to England when she was ten years old. Edith was born in England, but her father was nowhere in the picture. She had two younger sisters.

Bee often kept quiet, never revealing much to her friend. It was on one of those nights that Bee heard Edith's story. They all had different stories at St Augustine's: early sexual encounters, often first time, resulting in unplanned and unwanted pregnancies; sexual abuse by a family member or friend of the family or even a priest; and being shamefully cast out of their homes and hidden somewhere until the baby was born.

"My mother kicked me out after she found me vomiting in the toilet." Edith told Bee one night. "She knew I was pregnant before me. 'Two hens cannot live in the same pen!' She said. Packed my things and put them by the door!"

Edith had been raped by her mother's boyfriend when she was fourteen. Edith looked older than her age. She was tall and had the well shaped body of a grown woman. Her mother worked nights at an orphanage. One night while her mother was on duty, Edith's stepfather raped her. She knew her mother would not believe her so she kept her mouth shut. She was three months pregnant when she came to the hostel. Edith had two months to go before the baby was born.

"I am not keeping this baby! I am giving it away."

Bee stayed quiet, thinking on her own situation. She knew what would come next. Edith would want to know how she got pregnant too. She has not told anyone about it. She didn't even know what to tell.

"How could you give away your baby? I want to keep my baby," Bee said, remembering the conversation with Matron about the option for adoption. She had not even thought about it really: how it was going to work. All she knew was she was pregnant and the baby was hers. It was inside her. Living in her, breathing inside her, growing inside her. It was hers. Hers to keep. Matron said if she chose to keep the baby, she could stay at the hostel up to six months after the baby was born. She would get help and support needed to look after the baby. That would give her time to finish her education and look for work. "But think about it. It is not easy to bring up a child on your own. You are just a child yourself. Your baby could have the chance to be with a good Christian family who are capable of providing a good home to the child. Please think about it. You have your life ahead of you. A child would only hold you back. There's no shame in that Bee. You are still just a child."

Matron admired Bee's determination and hard working ethics. She knew there had to be much more to this girl's story than she had been told. A young girl shipped from her homeland to this country at the age of twelve and pregnant! With no family or anyone. To date, there had been no communication from anyone. She could only guess that the foster parents thought it best to cut all ties with the poor girl. But Bee was such a serious girl; she had no doubt that Bee would make it, whatever her choice.

"Somebody raped you Bee?" Edith asked, with her usual bluntness. Bee had shared some of her past with Edith: that she had lived with a missionary family; that they had sent her off to England when they found out about the pregnancy. But Bee had kept the details of her mysterious pregnancy to herself.

Bee froze. She tried so hard to erase from her memory the events of that night. She now understood a bit more about how a woman got pregnant and about babies, from listening to the girls sharing their stories. She knew what happened to her that night was not a dream. Pieces of memories from that night lodged themselves in little crevices in her mind. Sometimes just a thought, something said, an image, a smell, would dislodge a fragment from its hiding place, to roam around Bee's head, searching for an opening to escape. But somehow she managed to retrieve and suppress it. This time, it found an unlocked door and Bee had to set it free, by telling her story.

"Somebody came into your room twice and you didn't see who? You don't know who raped you?" Edith had heard all kinds of stories about rape but she could not believe what she was hearing.

Bee was still confused about that night. All she wanted to do was forget, everything about that night. She often wondered about Miss Florence and Mr David. How they just sent her away and never contacted her. She thought that perhaps it was because they didn't know where she was. She had written a letter to Miss Florence, letting her know she was moved to St Augustine's Hostel. She had written to her sister too. But she got no reply. One day a package arrived for Bee, which created some excitement amongst the girls. It was not something that happened often at the hostel. It contained everything Bee would need for when the baby came: a blanket, vests, socks, jumpers, mittens, booties and hats. No return address or name of sender.

"Bee, who could have come into you room like that? You know who did it, don't you?" Edith asked.

The brothers! Edith concluded. Bee realised then, she had not thought of them since she landed in England. It was as if they had somehow been erased from her memory.

"That's why they shipped you off, Bee. Because they know! That is why they never kept in touch! Wiped their hands of you. Bee! You listening to me?" Edith searched Bee's face for some response, but Bee was blank. "What you going to do, Bee? You shouldn't keep this baby! That will mess up your life!"

And as these memories escaped, so did all the tears, which had been bottled up since her last cry that night at the convent. Somehow she had managed not to worry about the future, just making it through each day of her new life. She didn't know any different. But the burdens of her reality were never far away

.

Chapter Ten

A t thirteen, Bee was the youngest at St Augustine's Hostel, yet she was so much more mature, more serious and disciplined than most of the other girls. It showed in the way she carried herself, how she managed her responsibilities. Chores were always done on time and with such care. Her side of the room was always neat and tidy. She applied herself to her education with remarkable interest and determination. Bee was conscientious and so considerate of others. Somehow this girl, from this tiny island Grenada, seemed to possess all of the qualities they were trying to instil in the other residents. For a thirteen year old girl, raped at age twelve, pregnant and shipped off like baggage to a strange country, with no family, not even a distant relative to call on, she was learning the ropes really fast and coping much better than anyone expected.

Bee was finishing a letter to her sister when Matron called her into the office. She had continued to write to her sister, even though she had not received any replies to any of her previous letters.

"Sit down Bee," Matron said, her voice softening, dropping the sharp edge with which she had to apply in order to set the boundary and keep order amongst the residents and staff. "A letter arrived for you this morning."

"A letter? For me?" Bee's entire self lit up with pure joy. Maybe it was from her sister. Bee had given up any hope of hearing from Miss Florence.

Bee was heading into her ninth month and in the last two months she seemed to have doubled in size. Her nose looked fatter, her lips thick, her hair continued to grow to alarming lengths as if fertilized by pregnancy. Matron used to feel sorry for Bee, having to carry such a heavy burden at such a tender age, but now she had such admiration for the girl. She knew enough to see how brave and courageous Bee was. Over the few months since Bee's arrival she had watched this young girl, who like many girls in her situation could have been challenged with mental issues. But instead she thrived and blossomed despite whatever adversity she had faced, with such dignity and grace. She was quick with her smiles, oblivious to her own strength.

"Yes. You have a letter from Grenada!" Matron said, looking at the return address on the back of the envelope. "From Bernadette George."

"That's me sister Matron." Bee said, reaching for the letter. She felt warm and happy all over. Finally! She could not wait to go to her room to read it.

"How lovely! Tell me about your family Bee. Your sister, how old is she?"

"She is nineteen years old Matron. She is my oldest sister. My brother is the oldest in all of us."

"You have any family over here? An aunty or an uncle?" Matron already knew that Bee had lost both parents and that she had lived with the missionaries who had sent her over to England.

"No Matron. I don't know." Bee answered. She started feeling a bit uneasy, like she did whenever she was forced to face her situation like that.

"So you have nobody at all here. Nobody, you perhaps could stay with after the baby comes?"

"No Miss. No Matron." Bee answered, shaking her head.

"Bee, does your sister know about the baby?"

Bee shook her head again, afraid of what might spill out if she opened her mouth. She took extra caution when she wrote to her sister, never to reveal anything about her pregnancy. They did not know anything about it. She continued to leave them with the story they were told: that she was in England for a better life, getting a better education, and all was well. She never let a word escape about what happened.

"Bee, have you thought about out little chat? Remember what I told you about the opportunity to have the baby adopted by a good family. Have you thought about it? I know a family who would love to have your baby. I can also try to help find you a family to stay with, Bee. You are still a minor. But no family will take you in with a baby. There is no shame in this, Bee. You can give up the baby and carry on with your life. You are not far away now, Bee. Think about it Bee. We want what is best for you. If you choose to keep the baby you will have our support. I promise."

Bee had thought of nothing more than what she was going to do. She did not know.

Later, in her room, Bee tore open the red and blue striped envelope with childish glee and great anticipation. She remembered how happy Miss Florence looked those times when she received letters from England. How she left them unopened until she retired after supper, then opened them carefully and settled to read them with such ceremony. They brought news of the family she left behind. How those letters transported her back to her homeland.

How sad she sometimes looked, staring at the letter in her hands, with a kind of sadness and longing.

Bee had not had any news from home since she left Grenada. Nothing from Miss Florence nor Mr David. Sometimes in her quiet moments, when all work was done and she lay in bed, Edith sleeping soundly on the other side, her mind wandered back into that old house. She liked living there. Until that night.

Bee read the letter quickly, devouring it with homesick hunger. Then she re-read it, slowly, taking in all the news from home, like a long awaited treat. *Everybody was ok. Her younger sisters were doing well in school. Bernadette was working in the village shop and housekeeping for the Reverend and his family. Her older brother got married to Isabel, the one who had a baby when she was fifteen, right under she Seventh Day Adventist father and mother's nose. Then they locked her away to pay penance for she sinful ways. Now we find out is John's baby and he didn't even know. But God is good. He made an honest woman of her now. They had a nice little wedding in the church. The child was three years old and never been outside in she life. But the strangest thing was how the missionaries just packed up and left the island. Just like that. Right after they sent Bee away. Said it was a family emergency. They just gone, just like that. She was so glad to hear that Bee was happy and getting on well in England. How she wish she could come to England too. But who going to send for her? And if she goes, who going to look after the younger ones? Anyway, she hoped Bee would get a good job soon so she could help them out. Maybe send for her sisters one day. May the good Lord bless her soul.*

May the Good Lord bless her soul.

Bee sat on the bed mulling over her sister's news and staring at the wall. The October dampness crept across the wall, spreading around the window. The room smelt of dampness, a mouldy smell that fills your nostrils, your head; winter had stripped the trees naked, making them look dead, their leaves rotting beneath them. This time back home it would be rainy season: everything green; the pungent smell of wet nutmegs, cocoa and cinnamon mingling in air; the breeze cooling off after the dry season; mango season finished, peas and sorrel blossoming and fruits soaking in rum and black wine, getting ready for Christmas.

Bee folded the letter, letting every word sink in, especially the part about the missionaries fleeing the island. Miss Florence had been in England all the time? She had promised to visit, but she had not even written Bee a letter. They were God fearing people, living by the commandments and the lessons of the Bible: be kind and honest; respect your elders; speak the truth and speak it always. "The truth shall set you free." That was what Miss Florence had told her over and over. The truth shall set you free. It was her truth which made them send her away like that and her truth which later chased them away.

Bee clasped her hands on her enormous belly and said the Our Father. Inside her, the baby kicked, a reminder of her truth. She did not feel free at all.

Chapter Eleven

On the thirteenth of November, in the very early hours of a cold and wet autumn morning, Bee went into labour. She had no idea what to expect. Edith had told her about her experience giving birth. "It just felt as if I wanted to poo, so I went to the toilet. If it wasn't for the nice Jamaican nurse, I would have had the baby in the toilet! It almost slipped out into the toilet!" It sounded so easy for Edith. She was a big girl, big all over. Everything seemed easy for Edith.

Matron took Bee to the London Hospital in Finley, Whitechapel, in case there were complications. There were two nuns and a Jamaican nurse in the delivery room with her. She could tell by the accent. She wondered if it was the same nurse who had delivered Edith's baby. Bee tried to do as she was instructed by the Jamaican nurse, breathing, pushing when she told her to. It was as if this baby, who had taken over her body for months such that she hardly recognised herself, wanted to take away her life too. Bee felt as if she were being ripped apart. She was sure she was going to die. Pain surged through her body with such force, knocking her out of herself, so she did not know herself anymore. After six hours of pushing and bawling, praying for her God to save her, she heard the most piercing cry of her baby. She heard the nuns say something about the afterbirth. Then she felt a warm gush and something slipped out again. She was sure the baby had ripped her open.

After her conversations with the Matron, Bee had thought about it. She tried to imagine her life after giving birth, giving away her baby, leaving the hostel, but she could not. She didn't know about the English ways, all this talk about being ready, preparing oneself for things to come. When her mother died, her sister just took over, caring for them the way she knew how. When the missionaries took her to live with them she just had to go live with them, do as she was told. Later, when they sent her away to this country, she had no say. No explanation was necessary when you were a child, because you had no choice nor any say in any matter. All Bee knew was how to carry on from day to day. And that is what she had done so far. It made life so much easier. She knew no other way. She observed the other residents closely, how some of them complained, sulked, sought attention, the hugging, consoling, anger, outbursts, breaking down in moments of distress. She didn't know those ways. Bee had so much to learn, but she knew enough to know the difference between dreams and reality. She did not think about the future, it was too far away. Her reality was life at the hostel: the residents, the liveliness, the cooking, cleaning, classes, girls chattering or arguing, babies crying. She recognized the look of frustration as the girls tried to cope with sick, crying, messy, hungry babies, but there was laughter too. Most of the girls opted for adoption, for various reasons. However, there was always great excitement when a brave young mother walked into the hostel, her new bundle in her arms, looking tired, yet so satisfied with the novelty of a new baby. For those who were forced to return, soft swollen bellies, breasts heavy with milk, but empty handed, the pain engraved on their faces spoke clearly and deeply of their loss. Bee had seen it on Edith's face too. Heard it a few nights in her crying, but

Edith quickly checked herself, toughened her skin to face her reality. Her mind was made up. She put it behind her, pretended it did not matter. "I don't even know what she looked like, Bee. But she will have a better life than what I can give her. I don't even have anything for myself, what can I give her, eh?"

"It's a little boy," the nun said, holding the baby, wrapped in the little cream blanket, out to Bee. "He's a good size baby. Six pounds, seven ounces!"

Bee was still raw from the pain, and feeling weak and tired, when the Jamaican nurse brought the baby. The smell of blood and Dettol made her feel sick. Bee hesitated. Six pounds seven ounces! That was not big at all. He looked so tiny, all wrapped up and fragile, that Bee was afraid to hold him.

"Come now, take him. Don't worry child, he won't break." the Jamaican nurse said. Nurse Angie. That was what Bee had heard the nuns calling the Jamaican nurse. She was nice looking. She had dimples in her cheeks and slanted, smiling eyes. She fixed the baby in Bee's arms. "See! He won't bite either." She laughed. Bee tried to smile. She held the baby closer, a bit awkward at first, but soon she had him snuggled to her. She felt a tingle in her breast as his new born scent filled her head, comforting her. What life can she give a baby, Bee had wondered at the time, but the instant she looked into his face she felt something she had never experienced before, something so pure and sweet and natural. This little wrinkled, *scald-crayfish* face baby - eyes closed but twitching, cherry pink lips sucking on something sweet but invisible, his tiny fists cuffed tight - was hers. This whole new little person that just came from inside her. He was hers. He had nobody else.

The older nun looked at Bee with sympathy. She was the midwife. God has called her to do his works delivering babies, not to judge. But looking at the young girl, she could not help wondering about the circumstances surrounding the birth of this little baby boy. She could not help questioning God's reason for casting such a heavy burden on one so young.

"Sister, you nuh find this baby looking real pale? Ah find he skin look a bit yellow? " the Jamaican nurse said, peering into the baby's face, then peeling away the blanket to examine him closer. In Jamaica, when babies were born so pale, the doctor always said the baby had jaundice.

Sister moved closer. She opened the baby's eyes with expert thumb and forefinger, pressed the skin on his arm, his chest, his face, softly, but firmly enough to make small dimples which slowly puckered back to the natural form.

"Yes. He's a bit on the pale side, but his eyes are bright and beautiful," Sister said, fixing the blanket around the baby. "He's a healthy baby."

"Well, when you go home, sit by the window, let him get some sunlight anyway. Just in case." the Jamaican nurse told Bee as soon as Sister left the room. "'Cause unless dis chile's fadder is a white man, he too pale!"

Bee froze! Held her breath. Held the baby a bit too tight. He cried. Opened his eyes a little. Closed them again.

"You a'right chile? You have a name fee him yet?"

Bee shook her head. Name! Bee never thought about names. She didn't think about things like that. She did not think about anything ahead.

"Well you have fee call him somet'ing. Now let me show you how to put the baby on you breast." She showed Bee how to hold the baby and place his mouth on her nipple. Lucky for Bee, she had long pointed nipples. The baby latched on as if he had done this several times, his mother's breast replacing that invisible sweetness he was suckling when she first saw him.

"See! Like he know breast long time! He is a natural." The nurse smiled. "Get some rest chile. You need it! Me name is Nurse Angie. Anything you need, ask for me. Ok?"

The girls looked so relaxed nursing their babies, but the little shooting pains she was feeling as the baby sucked made her wince. Looking at the baby, her heart swelled. It felt like it would burst with this overflowing of emotions. If somebody asked her how she was feeling, she would not know how to explain it. She had never felt like that before. One thing was sure, Bee was keeping her baby. Nurse Angie popped in to check on her that morning. She felt something for the child, something that took her back twenty years to Jamaica, when she was fourteen years old and pregnant. Her baby was given away and she was shipped off to England to live with her aunt. To hide the shame she had brought on her family. That happened a lot amongst West Indian families, but she had seen much more shameful things. What was so shameful about having a baby? She was in love with the baby's father, but he went away to join the British army. She never saw him again. He knew nothing of the pregnancy. She could not help wondering about Bee's situation. What a brave girl! Only thirteen, yet braver than a lot of grown up married women whose babies she had delivered.

Nurse Angie pondered about the baby. The child was so light skinned. Her suspicions grew thicker yet, after the surprise visit the baby had that morning while Bee slept. This white woman showed up saying she was there to see Bee, but looked so relieved when she was told Bee was resting. Nurse Angie had looked on with curiosity at the way the woman had stared at the baby, cocking her head this way then that, as if trying to figure out a puzzle. Leaning closer to the baby, peering into his face as if somehow her answer was wrapped up in that blanket with him.

Bee was awake when Nurse Angie popped in to check on her before finishing her evening shift, sitting on the bed nursing her baby as if she had done this before. Angie felt a little pang of longing and a tinge of envy. She had not been blessed with another child. Sometimes she thought God was punishing her, and wondered how life could play some cruel tricks on people. But at thirty five, she still had hopes. Angie recalled the earlier visit, wondering whether she should say anything to Bee, but something stopped her. Perhaps it was the way that lady left, so abruptly and in such a hurry, as if not to get caught. And that profound sadness in her smile. There must be a reason she did not want the girl to see her, and Nurse Angie did not want to stir anything unnecessarily.

"So you decide on a name yet?" she asked Bee.

"John Johnson Junior. I will name him John Johnson Junior," Bee said, smiling at her baby.

The nurse laughed; a friendly laugh. Not at Bee. "That's triple J! Are you sure you want to load up dis baby with dis big name?"

"That was my father's name Nurse. I want to name him after my father."

"That's a strong name. I like it." She winked at Bee.

" Ah see you going home tomorrow. You'll be aright chile. Jus' don't forget to give him some sun," Nurse Angie told Bee, although she knew, if her suspicions were right, sun was not going to make much difference to the child's skin.

Chapter Twelve

F lorence called St Augustine's Hostel right after her visit to the hospital. Upon returning to England it was not difficult to locate Bee. Wanting to check how Bee was getting on, Florence anonymously made contact with the matron. Then it was even easier to get information about Bee's delivery. As soon as Florence set eyes on the baby she knew straight away, without a doubt. She was dizzy from the sheer force with which this recognition slapped her in the face. This baby was her grandson. What she saw in the baby's face - his pure, angelic innocence - brought it all back and jolted her reality.

Over the months after Bee's departure, Florence had been watching her family closely. How impatient David had become, his steps slowed down, his shoulders slumped by an invisible weight. However her initial niggling suspicions about David's occasional absence from their room at nights transferred to her sons, when the boys' behaviour changed so dramatically. They became distant and sullen, quick tempered and defensive. The family was growing apart and she had to take action. Returning to England was not a difficult decision for any of them.

The truth about what really happened to Bee that night was still not clear, better to let sleeping dogs lie, yet it had haunted Florence since that night. The shame she felt was unbearable. God sees and knows all things. She could not live with herself if she did not try to make amends.

Florence prayed. *Please Father, forgive me. Forgive my family for our sins and transgression. Help me to make amends for our wrong doing. Help me to redeem this family and do what is right in your sight.* The boys knew nothing about Bee's situation and she intended to leave it that way. God was a merciful God.

All of the girls' wellbeing was very important to Matron. Her own mother had given birth to her in a home for unmarried mothers and was forced to give her up for adoption. She knew about those establishments. Many of them were operated by the church as Baby Farms. She had heard about the atrocities which took place there. Stories about how inhumane they treated the pregnant mothers, unjustly punishing them for crimes committed against them, for things that were not their responsibility. They made simple human mistakes, with no option to correct them or a shot at a second chance. She had worked in a few of them herself and had seen the evil which human, Godly people were capable of. When she was hired at St Augustine's Hostel, which was founded by the Salvation Army, she had vowed to make a difference, and she was determined to follow through.

Matron had to admit that she had a tender spot for Bee. She had watched how Bee fitted into her role of motherhood so naturally. She was coping so well with Baby JJ and managing to get all her chores and studies done. Bee spent a lot of her time in the kitchen, learning to cook with keen interest. Nothing was too difficult or too much for her to handle, no pot too big or too burnt to scrub, nor sink too overflowing with dishes for Bee to clean. As the old people said: *"Is only the eyes afraid of work."*

The cooks often played the radio, singing along with the popular sixties hits, so before long Bee was singing along with Millie Small's *My Boy Lollipop*, the Beetles *Can't buy me love* and *I want to hold your hand.* The songs made their way into Bee's repertoire, she was always singing while she worked. They never replaced the hymns she learned in church, though. Bee was a living example of the vision Matron had for the young mothers who passed through St Augustine's Hostel. And she intended to do all she could to help the girl and her baby.

When the Missionary lady had contacted the hostel, making enquiries, Matron did not make much of it. When she came to the hostel the day after Bee delivered her baby, expressing her desire to adopt the baby - although Matron wished that Bee would re-consider adoption - she couldn't help being suspicious about why this lady was so interested in Bee's baby.

"Our sons are growing up so fast and God wants us to share our blessings with the less fortunate." The lady said. And as if reading Matron's mind, that out of so many unfortunate girls at St Augustine's' why Bee, she continued. "We have heard about the girl being from the West Indies and having no family here. And she's so young, the poor child. You see, we were based in the West Indies for a few years and so we feel a special connection with the islands. So when we heard about this girl we knew God wanted us to do something to help." Florence begged God to forgive her as she spoke these words, she begged God to forgive her as she lied for a good cause.

How did they hear about Bee, Matron wondered. But she did not ask. They needed whatever help they could get and she wanted to help Bee find a good family if she chose to give up the baby. Who better than a Missionary family!

"We do have a request. We understand the girls can stay here up to six months after having their babies. Is that so?" The lady asked.

Matron nodded. At St Augustine's the girls were taken in at any stage during their pregnancies, however they were given up to six months after having their babies. Most of those who chose the adoption path and had family to return to, left soon after. Some were cast out of the family because of the shame and stigma attached to pregnancy out of wedlock. They were denied access to housing so they were placed in bedsits. If they were lucky, some found jobs, perhaps a husband and alternative accommodation.

"Due to the circumstances, and in the event that we cannot adopt the baby, we are requesting that you allow the girl to stay here until she finishes her studies and is old enough to work. Or until she chooses to leave of her own free will. We will make monthly contributions to the hostel, which I am sure would be very helpful," Florence proposed.

Even with her suspicions, Matron was very pleased with the way this was going. The running of the hostel depended heavily on donations from benefactors and other supporters. This was great news for St Augustine's and for Bee. The lady appeared to be sincere and from a good, God fearing family.

Two weeks after the Missionary lady's visit, Bee sat in the office in front of Matron once again, a very regular occurrence as Matron always seem to have something to discuss with Bee.

"How you getting on with Baby JJ?" Matron asked Bee, already aware of the girl's exemplary achievements and discipline. She had been observing Bee with the baby and her admiration just multiplied.

"Fine Miss. He's sleeping now." JJ was a calm baby. He nursed very well and slept most of the time, giving Bee chance to get on with her other responsibilities.

"Bee, have you given some thought to what we spoke about? To adoption? We had a visit from someone recently, showing interest in adopting your baby"

Just the mention of the word tugged on Bee's heart a little. She thought about a lot of things. When she lay in her bed at nights things ran around in her head, questions nagging, issues pushing themselves in the picture, causing her to worry. All she knew was that she could not give away her baby. Every time she looked at his little face, every time she held him, nursed him, she felt something soft and sweet in her chest. "Bee? This is a good family. They will take good care of Baby JJ. Give him a good life." As matron said those words, she wondered, not for the first time, what kind of people they were. After all, she had only just met the lady. She didn't really know anything about her?

"Miss I don't want to give away my baby." Bee said, finding her voice. "I not giving him away Miss." Bee sat looking at her hands, clasped in her lap.

"Bee, this family are people of the church. They can give Baby JJ a better chance at a good life. A good education. You are just thirteen! How will you look after him with no family?"

"I not giving away my baby Miss. I will look after him."

"Bee are you sure? Think about it."

"Yes Miss. I not giving him away Miss." Bee said and Matron saw the finality in her face.

"OK. Take some time to think about it Bee. Let's give it three weeks, then come back and tell me how you feel then. Whatever your decision, Bee, remember you have my support.

"Thank you Miss." Bee said.

Matron already knew her answer would be the same, whether it was three weeks or three months from now. She would do all she can to help Bee. With such dedication, discipline and diligence, Matron had no doubt that Bee was a survivor.

Chapter Thirteen

B ee was in the park with JJ, near to the little flat which she rented, when she met the first man she let into her life. It was the last day in July, a warm summer day, and everyone seemed to be in good spirits, sunbathing, picnicking or just sitting around, eyes closed, as if giving thanks for the lovely day.

Matron had kept her promise to the missionary lady, keeping Bee on at the hostel until she turned sixteen. Every month, the hostel received the pledged donation from the missionary family. Each time, she put aside the promised one pound fifty pence, into the fund which was opened by the Lady for Baby JJ. Bee worked as an assistant cook and did whatever was needed around the hostel, especially with initiating the new residents at the hostel.

When Bee turned sixteen, Matron found her a job in a local cake and biscuit factory. She then helped Bee to move into a bedsit. Within a year of working at the factory, Bee was promoted to Trainee Supervisor. Her manager, who was due to retire after thirty years with the company, was very impressed with Bee's work ethics. She was diligent, disciplined, as well as being a good motivator. "We have been watching you, Bee. You are such a hard worker, you have never been late nor have you missed a day's work. You are a great example to the other workers and we would love you to come on board the manager's team." Bee didn't know what it meant for her, but she worked alongside her manager and grew into the role, much like she did throughout her life.

Bee worked as much overtime as she could, and with her raise in salary she was able save up enough to rent her own little flat and finally move out of the little bed sit the council had given her. The other ladies at the bedsit were messy, always leaving pots and pans unwashed, and she ended up cleaning the mess she did not make. 'Cleanliness is next to Godliness' the Matron always drummed into their heads. And back in Grenada, she was always the cleaner of the house from the time she could remember. So when she saw the "For Rent. Female Only" sign posted on the house, she enquired right away.

The flat was an extension of a big house belonging to an old lady called Mrs Gladstone, who wanted to rent the flat to someone who would be able to help her with errands and cleaning as part of the agreement. Bee had her deposit saved and with excellent references from Matron and her manager she was able to rent the small apartment and buy her own furniture. She shared the one small bedroom with JJ. The kitchen and bathroom were tiny but big enough for them. And there was a storeroom which Bee could convert into a bedroom for JJ once she moved all the stuff from it. Bee felt so lucky to have found this flat. It was one bus stop away from her work, and five minute's walk to JJ's nursery school, and a park in the middle of the square with trees, swings and climbing frames, where she could take JJ, who was a bright and lively little boy. It was as if God was giving her extra blessings, making it up to her for being forced into this role of motherhood and adulthood far too young.

The sun was out in full glory and Bee had a day off. It was her birthday so she picked up JJ a little earlier from nursery and took him to the park. JJ played well with the other children. He loved the swing and Bee often struggled to unlatch him from it when it was time to go home. Bee sat in the shade under a tree, reading a novel she had borrowed from her landlady. Mrs Gladstone had quite a collection in her library, which she let Bee borrow whenever she liked. Bee was fascinated by the classics, especially by the Bronte sisters. She had read *Shirley* and *Wuthering Heights* by Charlotte and was reading Emily's *Jane Eyre*, for the second time. She loved getting lost in a world so different and far removed from the world she knew.

"Good afternoon," a male voice said.

"Afternoon," Bee said, looking up from her book into the face of the man standing a few yards away from her.

"Nice day eh! Have I seen you here before? Do you live around here?" He asked.

"Um hm. I live near here." Bee smiled. She didn't often engage in conversations with men, but he had a very friendly face. "I never seen you here before either."

"I live just across the square. You come here often?" His smile lit up his face. He was well built; with muscles of someone who did a lot of heavy lifting, real manual labour. He was about mid twenties.

"As often as I get time, today is my day off."

"Well it's a lovely day for the park." The man said. His smile broadened, showing a mouth full of the most perfect teeth Bee had seen on a man.

"And it's my birthday so I am spending it with my little man." Bee felt silly as soon as she said it. She didn't know why she was telling all this to a man she just met.

He glanced around.

"He's on the swing over there." Bee pointed to where JJ was.

"I am on my way to the fish and chip shop. Can I buy you and your little man some?"

Bee hesitated for a moment. "Thank you very much. Let me give you some money," she said, reaching for her purse. She and JJ loved fish and chips but she did not want this man thinking she was in the habit of accepting favours so easily.

"Absolutely not! It would be a great pleasure to buy you lunch on your birthday. See you in a minute." He replied.

"I do not even know your name," Bee said, as he turned to go.

"Errol. I was named after that actor Errol Flynn," he said, flashing her that smile again, as if it was common knowledge to know who Errol Flynn was. Bee had no idea to whom he was referring.

Errol's mind raced like a domino player trying to figure out the next move as he walked to the fish and chip shop. He was a fast mover but also one of those romantic young men who came along once in a while, or as his mother put it, "once in a blue moon". After leaving the chip shop with cod, saveloy and a steak and kidney pie with three portions of chips, he quickly ran home, where he lived with his mother, fetched one of her table cloths, a few cups with knives and forks, a couple of plates, a bottle of Tizer and orange squash, then headed back to the park, his heart sparkling with joy.

When Bee looked up, she could not believe her eyes, there was Errol struggling to carry everything.

"Don't look so worried. All will be revealed soon."

Hands on hips and a smile on her face, she watched as he spread a white table cloth under the tree, then lay everything out: three plates and knives and forks, then the bottles of drinks and plastic cups and the food. The smell of fish and chips mingled with the pink cherry blossoms.

Curious about what was happening, JJ jumped off the swing and ran over to his mother.

"This is my son JJ."

" Hello young man." He said, ruffling JJ's soft brown curls.

" JJ, say hello to the Mister ." Bee told her son.

JJ bent his head. "Hello," he said shyly and hugged Bee's leg.

Errol dished out the food, poured the drinks and stood up with a pleasing smile, admiring his efforts.

"Well, happy birthday! May the good Lord bless you with many more," Errol said softly, looking at Bee with a tenderness. Tears welled up in her head, threatening to overcome her usual composure. Bee had never been in this position before. She focussed all her attention on her son and her job. She had never felt like that before, but she liked that warm goodness she was feeling inside.

They sat under the tree eating and laughing, exchanging stories of the past. Anyone seeing them together might think they were a real family. Errol explained that his mother and father lived at number 82 on the other side of the park and he was their last child so he still lived with them.

"So tell me Bee, how old are you today?" Errol asked. Bee looked mature; with nice, hefty breasts and a well rounded body, but too young to have a son that age.

"Eighteen years."

"Only eighteen! I thought you were older. How old is JJ then?" Errol asked with a look of surprise.

"He is four." She replied, and watched him do his mental arithmetic. Errol did not ask where JJ's father was. He took in the child's very light skin, dark brown eyes and soft curly hair - what his mother would call good hair - and figured he was mixed somehow. It was not unnatural to find young women with children, and no fathers in the picture.

Neither of them wanted their evening to end, but it was time for Bee to take JJ home.

"Would you like to go to Victoria Park on Sunday? There is a boating lake there. JJ would love it." Errol knew he was coming on too fast, but he felt good with this girl. Confident.

Not wanting to look desperate or show her true feelings Bee said, "If we are able to come, we will meet you under this tree 12 o' clock on Sunday. Is that okay?"

"That is a time and a date. Hope to see you on Sunday."

They shook hands and she headed home. Errol hurriedly collected everything. He felt very pleased with himself. He knew he had a tongue lashing coming from his Mum about dirty plates and grass on her white table cloth, but it was well worth it. The weekend couldn't come fast enough for Errol. He was hooked.

Bee walked home with JJ, savouring what had just happened. She did not understand this new feeling but it felt good and she felt happy. She too prayed for the weekend to come quickly.

Chapter Fourteen

By the time Sunday finally dragged in, Bee was really anxious. She had never been on a date in her life. What should she wear? The only place Bee got dressed up to go, outside of work, was to church. And didn't God say to "Render your heart and not your garment", so even going to church was not a big dress-up occasion for Bee. She always dressed nicely. She had collected quite a bit of clothes from donations at the hostel and Mrs Gladstone had given Bee some nice outfits from her daughter's wardrobe, so she did not spend lots of money on clothes.

Mrs Gladstone always talked about her daughter Grace as if she had merely gone on holiday and would be back any day. That was until the day she handed Bee the bag of clothes, and shared with Bee the loss of her daughter. She died of cancer at just twenty-five, the reason for her continuous grief and the drastic decline in her health. Bee listened to her stories about Grace with patience and compassion. Grace was born at a time when her parents had given up all hopes of having a child. She came as a blessing to them in their forties. She was a free spirit, lively and full of dreams for a better world. From the time she was a little girl she stood up for, and was prepared to fight for, every cause of human injustice and inequality. She was strong willed, and from the time she turned eighteen wanted her independence. That was why her father built the extension. That way Grace could have her own place but still be part of the family home. He did not want their only child too far away. When Mrs Gladstone looked at what was happening around her, she couldn't help questioning why God had give them such a beautiful blessing just to take it away so prematurely. She stopped going the church as soon as she buried her daughter. Mrs Gladstone was very pleased to have Bee around. Grace would be pleased that she was helping a less fortunate person. It helped her to start accepting and letting go - well at least with the clothes. And Bee was great company for an old woman. She was no longer a lonely old lady.

Miniskirts were in fashion. It was what women Bee's age were wearing. Black women were hot, pressing tight, stubborn curls, into temporary straightness, which soon rolled back to their originality. Bee had never done it. Between work and JJ she just did not have the time to spend on things like that, nor any reason to. But when Bee told her friend from work about meeting this man, Claudia came to the rescue, full of excitement, her pressing comb, rollers and her little makeup kit in hand. Claudia was from Barbados, short with a pretty face, big round eyes and a big bottom. She knew men loved that and used it to her full advantage. Claudia got so excited about everything.

"Gurl you have to knock this man out! He should never have eyes for another woman after today! Come nah. Sit down, hush you mouth and let me fix you up nice. Is your time gurl. All you do is work, work. And little JJ could do with a man in his life, Bee. "

Bee sat down laughing with the girlish excitement of an eighteen year old. She was still a teenager, even though life had forced her to grow up fast. But God had also blessed her with the kind of maturity she needed in order to handle her responsibilities.

"We just going to the park you know! Not getting married!"

"Well by the time I finish with you, you will be getting married!"

When Claudia finished pressing Bee's hair it covered her shoulders, straight and jet black.

"Look at this hair! Gurl, why you always hiding this nice hair under some damn hat! I wish God did bless me with nice hair like yours. How old you say you was again! Chutes man!" Claudia said, as she rolled Bee's hair around some big, pink, sponge rollers.

Bee settled for the navy blue pleated skirt that reached just below her knees (it belonged to Mrs Gladstone's daughter), a cream blouse with yellow flowers (that buttoned at the front), a grey cardigan over it, blue stockings and flat comfortable pumps. No heels for Bee. She liked to feel comfortable. And she never left the house without her umbrella, coat, hat and gloves, even in the summer. Just in case. She just hated her hands to be cold. You never knew when the weather was going to change, knocking temperatures to lows that brought chills and chased surprised bodies hiding in coats, so she was always prepared.

Bee did not dwell too much on how she looked, but felt pleased with the person looking back at her in the mirror. She dusted her face with some of the powder from the tin which Claudia brought and added a touch of lipstick, the shade nearest to her skin colour. Claudia insisted on a bit of eye shadow, but Bee put her foot down on that. No way. She did not want to look like some tart! She was only going to the park, not the movies!

Errol got up at 6:00 am, too excited to sleep. He wished he could fast forward the hours. First thing he did was consult his little wardrobe. He wanted to dress to impress, even though they were only going to the park. That called for a trip to the market. Everything he had seemed too old or just not right for the special occasion. Amazing what a young man will do for love, but he had to look his best. He went down to the market for nine and by the time he got back it was 11:30. Time was going at an alarming rate and he did not want to be late. He had to boil the kettle five times to have a proper bath. Then when he finally put on the new clothes, they just looked too new and dressy for the park, so after spending all that money and running up and down, he went back to a regular pair of Levi jeans and a Ben Sherman shirt from his wardrobe.

Bee was already in the park with JJ when Errol arrived.

"I see you on West Indies time," Bee said, smiling and checking her watch.

"I apologise," Errol said, slightly embarrassed. After wishing for time to speed up, he was still late. This was not a good start.

"It's ok," Bee reassured him. "JJ could never get enough of this park. He didn't mind waiting."

With that, they headed to catch the 277 bus to Victoria Park.

Errol and Bee sat under an oak tree while JJ ran around the park. He was absolutely fascinated by the lake with the ducks. He soon found a playmate, which Bee was relieved about. She tried to keep as much distance as she could between herself and Errol, but she felt pulled toward him by some force stronger than her own. And she was not the only one.

Meanwhile Errol was having mental conversations with himself. He had looked forward to this day with a boyish excitement and anticipation that he had never felt before. From the time they sat under the tree, all he wanted to do was pull Bee close to him and kiss her. Every nerve in his body wanted to touch Bee, make contact, but he tried to keep his urges under control. *Easy Errol. Easy. Take your time man. Don't move too fast man, you don't want to spoil your chances before you even get them!*

It was a lovely day; warm rays of sunshine touched milky white bodies sprawled around the lake, soaking in every bit they could. Children danced about with glee, happy to be outside and warm. Men sat on the edge of the lake, holding fishing lines. Young couples snuggled as close as they could with guarded discretion. And soon enough, pulled by that common force, Bee found herself leaning into Errol. Before she knew it, she was nestled into his side. Errol pulled her closer, gently, so her head rested on his shoulder.

That was the first of many afternoons in the park, the only kind of date Bee would go on because of JJ. Eventually, with lots of persuasion, together with Mrs Gladstone's offer to watch JJ, Bee agreed to the odd night at the movies. JJ was used to Mrs Gladstone. He often stayed with her when Bee worked extra hours.

Over the next few weeks love blossomed between Bee and Errol, like a tulip in springtime, as they shared laughter, jokes and kisses. They both went with the flow of the heart which was quickly becoming one. They enjoyed similar things in life. And for the first time since arriving in England, Bee felt really loved. Things were coming together in her life, her son was in a good school and they had settled into their little flat. Errol helped Bee to convert the storeroom into a small bedroom for JJ. She enjoyed her job and she was experiencing something she had only read about in novels and seen in the movies. But most importantly, Errol was good with JJ. and this put Bee's mind at ease. She had heard enough stories about step fathers and step mothers ill-treating children who were not theirs. Thank God Errol was different.

Errol left Jamaica when he was ten years old. His father had travelled to England, worked hard like most West Indians did. After the first year, he missed his wife so much he wanted to take her up, leaving Errol with his aunt. But she refused to leave Errol behind. As a child, her own father migrated to Cuba to work in the sugarcane plantation, leaving her mother with eight children to bring up on her own. They never saw him again. She remembered how much she missed her father. She was not leaving their only child behind just because everybody else were doing it. So she waited another year until they had enough money for both of them to travel together.

Bee was forced to share some of her story with Errol. He who found it a bit strange that she had no family in England, and that she was so young, with a four year old child. But he did not pry. Bee received the odd letter from her sister back home, and in return she wrote back, putting the occasional five or ten pounds in the envelope, which meant a great deal to her family back home.

Each night Bee went to bed with prayers on her lips for the blessings which God had bestowed upon her. And every morning she awoke with bigger hopes and dreams. And Errol on her mind.

Chapter Fifteen

One year after meeting Errol, and the courtship that followed their first date in the park, Bee discovered she was pregnant. This flooded her with memories of the circumstances surrounding her first pregnancy, but this time Bee experienced some joy. She had Errol and she was confident he would stand by her. It would be nice to give JJ a brother or sister.

When Bee told Errol the news, he was over the moon.

"We better get married then," he said.

"Is that the best you can do Errol?" Bee said, smiling as she mimicked this line from some movie she must have seen.

Errol was romantic, in his own way. In the way he knew how to be, but he did not have time to prepare. And all that fancy down on your knee kind of proposal belonged in the movies anyway. It was not his style.

"You will have to give me two cows and five chickens for my hand in marriage," Bee told him, laughing.

Errol held her to him, tight yet gentle, looking into her eyes with the kind of open tenderness that most of the men he knew from his background felt uncomfortable showing. Bee was not the kind of woman that men would consider sexy, even though she had a nice body, adequately endowed on the chest and backside. Bee was shrouded by a shyness and reserve which made her appear serious. But

God, he loved that woman! She had big, sleepy eyes and a rude mouth, with lips that looked out of place on her face, more suited on a bold, sexy woman. Lips that Errol itched to crush with his, to suckle and nibble tenderly, from the first time they met. Lips that set his groin red hot, every time he kissed her.

"I love you with all my heart, Bee," he said, swallowing the lump those words formed in his throat. He did not know how they escaped but was glad he got them out.

Bee fought back the tears his words evoked. She did not know how to proclaim her love with words. It was not something that came easily. She just knew her feelings for Errol were real. She felt his love and she knew he felt hers too. Being old fashioned, Bee had wanted to wait until they were married before having sex. She had never really experienced it the way it was meant to be. But what she and Errol had was strong. She knew Errol had a hard time stopping himself halfway. She was also afraid that he might go elsewhere if she did not surrender. Claudia was always talking about the men in her life and how good sex was for her.

"So you and Errol do it yet?" Claudia asked her one day, three months after she and Errol started seeing each other. When Bee told her no, Claudia could not believe it.

"Girl you better watch it. These West Indian men don't make joke you know. Especially these Jamaican men! They like their sex bad. If he en getting it from you, believe me, he gon get it from some other woman! I know what I'm talking about."

Up until that day, Bee had only let Errol kiss her. She let his eager hands roam over her breasts, with her bra still on of course. She let them wander down her belly, slide down her thighs, awakening in her something she never knew she possessed, as their bodies pressed onto each other's. She let his wayward hand climb up her thighs until he reached the middle, but every time that hand strayed, every time it started to creep between her thighs to explore further, she'd pushed it away and clamped her legs tight, as the demon from her past intruded. The first time Bee let Errol go all the way, she prayed for the will to banish the demon from her life. She asked God's blessings for the joy she wanted to let herself feel. Well God must have answered her prayers because that night He placed JJ in the hands of her friend for the night and Errol got a well-deserved night off, so Bee had no excuse. They had gone to see *To Sir With Love,* with Sidney Poitier. Bee even indulged in a bit of cider while Errol drank Guinness stout. And with her head a little tipsy, unshackled from the image of her son sleeping across the room, Bee let go and let Errol take her to a heaven she never knew existed. They awoke in each other's arms, refreshed and ready to share that journey once again.

Bee was religious enough to feel the weight of guilt which fell upon her. She was an unmarried woman and it was sinful according to the Bible. By this time they were spending every minute they could spare together. Errol was always round Bee's flat, but she never let him stay the entire night. Ms Gladstone did not seem to mind. He was quite a handy man and so she was always finding something for him to fix or some odd job for him to do around the house. And being the comedian he was, Errol always made Ms Gladstone laugh.

The next few weeks, the conversation was all about their hopes and dreams. Errol's love for Bee brought out the best in him. He was a great father to JJ who called Errol dad. Bee and Errol never discussed JJ's real father and because of

Errol's light brown skin, due to it was easy to assume he was JJ's father.

In July 1970, Bee and Errol got married in the local registry office and started a new chapter in their lives. The company Bee worked for had branched out all over the country and her responsibility grew with it. She was in charge of a team of over fifty fellow workers and earning a good wage. Errol also earned a good living as a crane operator on the local docks, where he unloaded sand from ships to supply the growing building trade. He worked every extra hour he got. *'By the sweat of your brow, you will eat bread.'* With their combined income, they were able to move into a three-bedroom house in Bow, which they rented from a Jewish man named Mr Massin. They were lucky. Even with the passing of the Race Relations Act in 1965 one still saw physical signs declaring 'No Blacks. No Irish. No Dogs', even though these were illegal. Racism was real; immigrants were still facing discrimination trying to rent properties. Mentally these signs still existed, and made things difficult for people like Bee and Errol. Lucky for them, Mr Massin was only interested in the colour of money. He was a Nazi victim, Russian by birth. He fled Germany at the outbreak of the Second World War, and invested his money in properties in East and North London.

Mrs Gladstone was sad to see them leave but Bow was not too far from Mile End, so she knew she was not losing them for good. She was proud to see how Bee carried herself and how she progressed in life. So young, yet she possessed a maturity and sensibility which far surpassed her youth. Good people like her did not come along often, especially with the prevalent and growing racism with which black immigrants were faced. She was very aware of the political climate, the injustices faced by black people. She knew her daughter would have been very proud too. The day Errol brought Bee and Baby Cicely home from hospital was the happiest day of his life next to his first date with Bee. Cicely was born at the London Hospital. She was a big baby: eight pounds five ounces, with a head of black curls and Errol's nose and complexion. Errol was in love with his little girl from the moment he held her in his arms. He loved JJ like his son, but Baby Cicely completed their little family. Be called her Ceecee.

Bee was even more attractive to Errol, all mumsy, full-breasted and ripe with milk. Errol loved to snuggle into her bosom whenever Baby Cicley gave him chance. She seemed to always be hungry. Unlike JJ, who slept most of the time, Baby Cicely spent most of her wakeful hours latched on to Bee's breasts. It was the only sure way to pacify her regular crying spells. But soon enough Bee was forced to introduce her to the bottle, in order to prepare herself for her return to work.

After two months of getting used to the new addition to their family, they settled into their routine. JJ was settled in his school, and Baby Ceecee stayed with a child minder who lived three houses away. Bee returned to work.

Chapter Sixteen

Bee received two letters which made significant changes in her life. The first one came from her brother in Grenada.

Dear Bee,

Greetings in the precious name of the Lord and Saviour, Jesus Christ, who has blessed you and has kept you over the many years like he did with Joseph in Egypt in the Bible and as Joseph, I believe it is for a purpose because Patsy, my daughter has passed all her exams and would like to come to England to study nursing. If you can help her by giving her accommodation, we will be so pleased because as you know, there is little opportunity for our bright, young people in Grenada and I will always be in your debt.

Your loving Brother

John.

Bee kept in touch with her brothers and sisters back home. At Christmas she always tried to send them a box with food stuff and other goodies for the family. It was a real novelty to get stuff from abroad. Her older sister, Bernadette, never got married nor did she have any children. She just never found a man she wanted to marry. One of the sisters moved to St George's to work at Kirpalani's Store. The other one had two children with an older man who had a shop in Grenville. And one brother travelled to America to harvest apples and never returned.

The oldest brother, John, was married with four children, Patsy was the oldest.

Bernadette often hinted at how nice it would be if the other sisters could get the opportunity to travel to England. Broken families were being patched together how and when they could, after being dismantled, separated by thousands of miles and oceans, for so many reasons; parents leaving children, children leaving siblings, aunties, uncles, grandparents. In many cases, difficult choices were made. Perhaps it was the fact that Bee was the youngest of them which relieved her from the expected obligation that would otherwise have bound her to fulfil their dreams of travelling abroad for a better life. But once the letter arrived, Bee felt she had to do something to repay the gratitude which she experienced for having achieved so much. She must help her brother's daughter.

When Errol got home from a night shift, Bee read him the letter. Errol did not have a single brother or sister and was not really in contact with the family back in Jamaica. He knew his parents sent money home at Christmas to his Aunt and other close relatives, and often contributed towards that. But he too felt they had to take this opportunity to help Bee's niece. He started formulating a plan. They were both earning decent wages. Errol worked as many extra shifts as he could get. The English drivers hated the night shifts and because the ships were mostly able to dock on the River Thames when the tide was low, often early hours of the morning, he covered lots of night shifts. Because of this, his company gave him a loan to buy a brand new Ford Cortina to get to and from work, because at the time, buses stopped running at twelve 'o' clock at night and didn't start until five in the morning.

"Let's see if Mr Massin would consider selling us this house. We could fix up the attic for Patsy to stay." Errol suggested. Until then, the idea of buying a house seemed inconceivable, but sometimes he allowed this dream to play around in his mind. This dream also had a place in Bee's mind, so she was relieved Errol was ready to take the chance. More and more West Indians were moving in that direction, buying old, rundown buildings and fixing them up to liveable conditions. They were already saving money. They were both part of a scheme called susu or pardner money. The scheme was run by local West Indians who could not get loans from banks or building societies. They devised their own lending. Every week each person in the scheme would put in the pot the same amount of money. Each week, one person, a different one each time, would get the whole pot. Errol and Bee were in three of these schemes and felt confident about being able to handle a mortgage.

When Mr Massin came round for the rent, Errol put the proposal to him. After a long discussion, many cups of tea and Bee's lovely homemade banana cake, Mr Massin said, "I will think about it and let you know soon as possible."

The day Mr Massin came for his rent, before he could even knock on the door, Bee flung it open with a big smile on her face. Errol was not at home.

"Good Afternoon Mr Massin. How have you been?"

"Good. Good, my dear. I've got good news for you and your husband, " he said, smiling. Bee invited him in for the customary cup of tea and chat.

"You made me think about my age. I am an old man now. It is time for me to cut down. I have no children to inherit all this. What am I to do with it all? I have a four-bedroom house in Poplar. Not too far from here. It needs some work of course, but you can fix it up. You have been very good tenants over the years so I will give you first preference and good price. Good, good price for you."

Bee was so moved she hardly heard a word Mr Massin was saying. She cried and hugged. "Mr Massin, Thank you! Thank you so much!" she said, over and over again. Mr Massin had never experienced this joy of giving and seeing and experiencing someone else's joy. Bee's reaction made him reach for his handkerchief.

"It's okay my child. The Lord has blessed me with so much, yet so little. I have no children. What will I do with it all! Your husband will have a lot to do. "

Bee was on a high. When Mr Massin left, she got down on her knees right there in the kitchen, with her arms held up in praise. "Thank you Jesus! Thank you Jesus! My God you are so good!" Bee lifted herself up with song and dance. She was glad no one was watching her because they would think she was crazy! When she couldn't dance anymore, Bee sat down and reflected on how far she had come, from being shipped from her home to this strange country she called home. .

Bee and Errol were busy putting plans together for the purchase of their property. They had enough for the deposit (saved from their susu hands) and were able to get a loan from the bank. Mr Massin had also agreed for them to stay in the flat for half the rent, while they renovated their new property. Errol got a few builder friends together. He was always the first to chip in himself in these situations, so that was easy enough. It was great to have this togetherness and willingness to help out a brother man in need. After all, they were all one people working together for the same cause. So just as they pooled together for their susu scheme, so they put their skills together, taking real estate into their own hands, making it easier for West Indian immigrants to own their homes. West Indian *maroon* style: with friends pitching in, they worked on the property. Errol and Bee supplied food, drinks, transport, whatever it took to get the work done fast: *taking night and make day- as West Indians say.*

It was while all this work was going on that the second letter came. It was from Matron at St Augustine's. Inside was another letter from Florence and a bank book. West Indians have a saying, "When God can't come, he does send." That was when Bee found out that Florence had tried to adopt JJ and that, through Matron, she had been making monthly contributions since he was born, into a fund in his name. Matron had remained in touch with Florence, passing on news about JJ's welfare over the years. The fund was supposed to be given to JJ when he was eighteen, however when Matron told her the news about Bee and Errol buying their own house, Florence instructed her it was time to hand it over to Bee. What better cause.

Bee unfolded the letter and read it carefully. She read it over and over, as painful as it was.

15th March 1974

Dear Bee,
Please forgive me for what might now appear to be an intrusion into your life after all these years. I have prayed to forget as much as I have prayed for forgiveness for the misfortune which resulted in the action which we were forced to take, in sending you off the way we did. Every day I prayed that the years would make it possible to forget, that each year it would get easier, but every day, I have been haunted by what has happened to you, and by the hands of a child from my very womb. I have prayed for God to guide and protect you and my grandson. Yes, that too I have

accepted. I pray, now that you are a mother yourself, you would be able to understand what it might have been like for me. And I ask with all my heart for your forgiveness Bee. Please forgive my family.

David has passed away. He had a heart attack while he slept. He has taken this to his grave without making peace and for that I am regretful. I am very ill myself. My doctor thinks it's cancer. This must be my punishment, but I have made peace with my God.

When my mother passed away, I inherited some money and have given some of this to my grandson. I may never meet him again, (I say again because unknowing to you, I had paid him a visit at the hospital) and I don't blame you, but I wanted him to have this contribution which I hope will be used towards his education and to help in whatever way which will benefit you as well. I have heard from Matron, (I hope you don't mind) how well you are doing and I feel proud of you for your strength and grace. May God be with you and your family.

Sincerely,
Florence

Enclosed was a bank book with the sum of £1500. After all those years of hiding this secret, of wondering and praying without even knowing why, the letter lifted a weight from her shoulders which she thought she was carrying well. It offered her the salvation she didn't even realize she needed. Bee refolded the letter. There was just one thing she had to do to release herself from this for good. She decided then to finally tell Errol the truth about JJ's birth

Bee and Errol threw a house warming and thank you party for all their friends who worked so hard to get the house ready in record time. Bee loved to cook and entertain so with the help of a few friends, she set about preparing the goat meat, rice and peas, salt fish fritters, sweet cake soaked in rum, and banana bread. DJ Big Red, one of Errol's friends, brought his sound system which he had made himself, like they used to build back in Jamaica. They invited friends, neighbours and work colleagues who came from all over East and North London. By 10:00pm the party was jamming- calypso and reggae filling the room, mingling with, the smell of curried goat and rice and peas. The music was so loud it could be heard from two blocks away, but no one complained. Black people had a reputation for being aggressive and having a chip on their shoulders but nothing could be further from the truth. The true situation was that they had to fight twice as hard to get ahead with all the racism they faced. And they were here to stay no matter what people threw at them, even if that meant having to physically fight their neighbour, work colleagues or even the shopkeeper, who used every opportunity to charge them above normal price.

The party went on until about 4am and all the food and the drinks ran out. They both were happy and very much in love. Life was good to them both, and above all they made a great team: Bee an excellent organiser and Errol a very hard and willing worker. They were looking forward to moving into their new home.

Chapter Seventeen

Patsy landed in England in 1976 full of spice and everything nice, one on a day in September when the weather couldn't make up its mind whether to stay warm a little longer or start getting ready for autumn. Patsy had just finished two years of upper school, which was like college, and had worked at a store in Grenville for a year and a half to help save up (together with what her father had put aside for her) to buy her ticket.

Bee and Errol had moved the family to their new home and had been living there for two years by then. JJ was twelve and Ceecee was five years old. Bee was very house proud. She had used some of the money which she got from Florence towards the furniture. It was the first time she was getting to choose her very own and Bee wanted their new home to look really nice.

In her letter to John, Bee had instructed Patsy to take the train to London and get off at Mile End Station, where Errol would pick her up. Errol was on the night shift and so he was too tired to get up in time to drive to the airport. It was easy enough and there were always people to ask for help. She was sure Patsy could do it. "Look out for a bright yellow car" Bee had reminded her.

Errol got there early to get a parking space outside the station. In those days, there were no traffic wardens and very little parking restrictions. The train was due at the station about midday so Errol got a newspaper and bottle of

Tizer and waited. At around twenty past twelve he saw this tall, slim young lady dragging a suitcase outside the station. Errol knew straight away. She looked the part of West Indian just come to London, but with some confidence. This must be Patsy. He approached her with a smile.

"Patsy?" He asked, taking in the good looking young lady standing in front of him, in her jeans and floral shirt under the grey coat which Bee had posted to her months ago. Her pretty face with her big round eyes and rude mouth, like Bee's, was framed by her short fashionable afro.

"Yes." Patsy looked up at the man enquiring. "Uncle Errol?" She smiled, recognizing him from the wedding photo her Aunt Bee had sent them. "I saw the yellow car earlier, but no one was in it." He looked even better than in the photo. Nice smile. Nice teeth.

"Sorry about that. I just had to nip to the gents."

"Nip to the gents?" Patsy looked at him puzzled.

Errol laughed. "The toilet."

He took the suitcase and one of the bags she was carrying and put them in the boot of the car.

"So I see you made it OK on the train," Errol said. When Bee told him about Patsy travelling by herself he was a bit concerned, recalling how daunting it was for West Indians travelling back in the sixties on airplanes for the first time, arriving in big countries for the first time, and experiencing a lot of first time shockers. But Patsy didn't look at all flustered by the experience.

"It was ok. Not the first time I riding plane you know. I been to Trinidad. I just asked for directions. Me not no country bookie you know! I have a tongue in me mouth." Patsy said, laughing lightly. She did not want Uncle Errol to think she was rude.

"Hm. I could see that my dear. I could see that!" Errol laughed. This one was no small island girl. He could see that already.

Pasty always felt she belonged in the city. Country life was too slow for her. She read a lot, devouring any piece of literature, soaking up the scenes in every magazine she could put her hands on, always imagining she was one of those people in them. She loved fashion and bright lights, so before Patsy even *set foot* on that plane, she had already travelled to all kinds of places in her head, in her dreams. She wanted to be an air hostess but her mother and father insisted she study nursing, like so many of the West Indian women who travelled to England.

The journey from the airport was not a long one. Patsy did not know what to expect. Her aunt Bee looked older than her age. She seemed so much more mature than Uncle Errol. And back home, everybody thought England was a place where everyone lived in big houses with everything and *drove motor cars,* but Patsy was shocked to see the size of house and how nice it was inside. The kitchen was nice and cosy. The sitting room was big, with a wall cabinet in the corner with all kinds of ornaments: framed photographs of Bee, Errol and the children at different stages and glasses for all occasions, collected over the years. The sofas and chairs were decorated with crocheted mats and a big bright rug covered the carpet which never got chance to see the light of day.

Bee prepared a good old-fashioned Grenadian dinner for her: Red Snapper with rice and peas. After dinner Patsy opened her suitcase, which her aunt Bernadette had packed with all the things she knew Bee could not get in England guava cheese, fudge, cinnamon, cocoa balls, ginger, sorrel, bay leaves, nutmegs, tonkabean and even some green Julie mangoes. The aroma took Bee right back to her little village, bathing in the river, climbing mango trees and playing in the road without any fear of oncoming traffic. It filled her with nostalgia and longing.

Bee took Patsy to the room they had prepared for her. It was simple, painted cream, big enough for a double bed, wardrobe, dressing table and a chair in the corner, by the window which let the sun shine in. Bee was happy they could offer her niece this opportunity. She recalled her own arrival in England, hidden away as if she has some kind of disease, then sent off again to the hostel without any explanation. But God had protected her and look how far she had come. Patsy was nothing like her. She looked like a very bright girl. Bee had no doubts at all that this young lady would be just fine.

Bee made sure Patsy felt at home. She was family. Luckily they were the same size so Bee gave Patsy some of her jumpers and other warm clothing, but she knew that as soon as Patsy was able to, she would be discarding them for younger, more fashionable stuff. She could already see that her niece was no simple country girl.

Patsy's arrival brought more that the aroma of spices into their new home. With them came the memories of home. Bee sometimes wondered what happened to those brothers. She did not think of them by names, but just as the two brothers. But this time the memories were different. This time she could let them go without too much agony, just as they had come. Bee was relieved she had opened up to Errol about JJ. She did not want any secrets between them. And as far as JJ knew, Errol was his father and no one questioned or took time to calculate how old JJ was and how long Errol and Bee had been together. She had made up her mind to take only the positives with her to build her future on and Errol's understanding and support made it so much easier. Besides that, family members who were left behind with grandparents were being sent for after two or three years. It was very common in those days for instance, for a brother to turn up out of the blue, and then two years later, a half-sister. Some of them would meet brothers and sisters who were born in England for the first time. Though many of them felt like nomads, going to England to make something of themselves was The Dream. As if life meant nothing before embarking on this trip across the ocean.

Chapter Eighteen

Patsy settled into life in London as though she had been there longer than Bee and Errol. She was the kind of person who would strike up conversation with just about anybody, so she made friends easily. She was larger than life and the heart and soul of any group, so before long Patsy had a good circle of friends from many of the islands. She studied hard and partied even harder.

There was a growing band of young, gifted and black people, determined to make a success of their newfound life. And even with all the prejudice and racism which they faced, they had come too far to let that stand in their way. So when the first and second generation Caribbean people found themselves excluded from the pubs and clubs, they started their own entertainment. They held blues parties in friends' basements, to keep the noise down. Some of the speaker boxes were as large as wardrobes and they were handmade to get as much power out of them as possible. Some of her young white friends with whom she studied were huge fans as well. The close dancing, 'The Rub', was very sexual and the bass was like a large heart beating and vibrating.

Bee was busy with work and the children, leaving home on mornings when Errol and Patsy were just getting in from their night shifts. Patsy was training at the local hospital and night shifts were part of her training. So it was not unusual for Errol and Patsy to arrive home around the same time on mornings, when Bee and the children were leaving the house.

Errol and Patsy began spending the mornings together, having breakfast, chatting about work and life. Ten minutes turned into half an hour, lengthened into an hour, two hours. Patsy was getting to know Errol better than her Aunty Bee. When Bee was at home, Patsy was at work, out with friends, or at some party. Bee was so happy to see her niece fitting in and coping so well, she just let her get on with her life.

Patsy felt so comfortable with Errol that their conversations change from the everyday stuff to more personal things. On one of these mornings, their usual time at the kitchen table somehow relocated to the bright orange settee. It was so big it took up a whole side of the sitting room. That room was only used when they had visitors, and on very rare occasions, when the family might end up in there for some kind of celebration. Whether it was chemistry or fate, Errol and Patsy, house to themselves, were somehow pulled to a more comfortable setting.

"Uncle Errol can I ask you something? Don't laugh eh?" Patsy began. But as soon as the words came out, she began to get nervous. Back home people didn't talk about personal things in the open so it was difficult for her. She had so many questions. She tried to open the conversation from all different angles. It was not shyness. Patsy was not at all shy nor was she an innocent. But it was what she felt for Errol, her aunt's husband, which held her words.

"Listen," Errol said. "We have talked about almost every subject under the sun. Whatever it is you want to ask me, just ask. Don't try to dress it up or season it, man. Just give it to me raw."

"Okay, okay. Not to laugh at me you know," Patsy said, blushing.

"Ah won't laugh man. Cha!" Errol put on his serious face.

"Well, I am still a virgin," Patsy blurted.

Errol's eyes widened. He too had his own attraction brewing. He wondered where this was going. He shifted his position, feeling a bit uneasy. Almost afraid.

"Well I don't want to get pregnant young like most of my friends back home and so far it worked for me," Patsy continued. She knew of her own mother's pregnancy with her at fifteen. She had overheard her mother talking about it to her friend. Patsy was not stupid. It didn't take rocket science to work out her Aunt Bee's age when she had JJ.

Errol sat quietly listening to Patsy. This conversation was making him nervous too. He and his mates talked about sex all the time, but it was not a subject he touched on with women. And certainly not with his wife's nineteen year old niece. He remained quiet, but held his mind wide open for wherever this was going.

"You know that feeling you get when you dancing *The Rub*? Well the music does take over my whole body. And I does get these feelings when I dancing with boys. Sometimes when I go to bed, I still on a high, feeling as if the music still pumping inside my head. It does make me feel real sexy. And I does wish the singer could do what he singing about to me."

Errol tried to stay cool. Heat rose in his groin. He had his own pumping going on and he must tread carefully.

"You think I am crazy eh?" Patsy said. Just talking about this to Errol, the two of them there alone like that, she was feeling her own music.

"Nah! How I could think you crazy? The Rub is a sexy groove, and when you feel music you suppose to feel good."

Errol didn't know how to approach this. Growing up nobody talked about feelings or anything you wanted to know about. You just felt things, heard things and learnt things as you went along. But this young lady was bold and bright as daylight.

"Believe it or not, this feeling you feeling is as natural as breathing. Hm. Everybody goes through these things. A lot of people go on like it's unnatural, so we fight it and sometimes we make the wrong choices. But it is a feeling we need to express with the right relationship. The right person. Not just for fun or for one night"

Back home, all Patsy heard was *don't play with boys or you will get pregnant. And you sure going to Hell because the Bible says fornication is a sin*. So it puzzled Patsy that so many women had several children with different men but not married to one. And how many children had half brothers and sisters all over the island? Patsy was always regarded as a forward girl. She was always asking questions, even though they said children should be seen and not heard.

Feeling a bit more comfortable with the conversation, Errol continued.

"Well you're a damn good looking girl Pat. So you have to be careful. A virgin is a trophy for a lot of guys so don't give it away to any guy. You want to wait for that special guy and that special moment. Remember you can only lose it once. Don't sell it cheap or give it away for next to nothing. Treat it as a special gift for the one you love."

Patsy wanted to continue the conversation with many questions exploding in her head but Errol had given her enough to think about for the moment.

"I off to catch some sleep yeah." Errol said and left the room fast before the rising bulge betrayed him.

The discomfort which drifted around them the next morning went unnoticed. Bee was too busy getting on with life; being wife, mother, aunty, friend. She was occupied with making sure everyone was happy at work and at home; that JJ and Ceecee were doing well at school, being brought up in the church and did not miss out on anything that she never had access to as a girl.

Chapter Nineteen

I t was Patsy's birthday so she arranged a night out with her friends at a club down the City of London called *The Bird's Nest*. It was on a Saturday night so she thought it would be a good idea to invite Bee and Errol along. They were not that much older than her and it would be nice for them to meet some of her friends whom she worked and hung out with.

They were having breakfast, something they rarely got to do together, when Patsy invited them.

"Can you see me on the dance floor like some sixteen year old? I only used to dancing to church music and maybe the odd calypso, but this modern thing they call pop or soul is not my cup of tea." Bee said.

"Come on Aunty Bee. You two always working, working. Take a break. You and Uncle Errol could do with a night out man." Patsy said. Trying to convince them.

"Errol could go if he wants, but not me. Besides, I have to get up for church on Sunday morning." Bee never missed out on church.

"What about it Uncle Errol?" Patsy asked, with a grin on her face. Almost challenging him. Secretly, she hoped he would come.

"Why not? I could come along and show you youngsters a thing or two on the dance floor. You know what my friends used to call me? The Caribbean James Brown."

Bee burst out laughing. "The only split you can do is in your trousers when you sit on your fat behind."

Errol smiled. Bee had never really seen him in action. They never went to parties, except at friends' house and that was different. "We will see. Remember he who laughs last laughs the longest. Go ahead and laugh. You will see."

"Hm. Well I would love to be a fly on the wall to see you in action Errol." Bee laughed. She knew Errol could dance. She didn't know any Jamaican who could not hold their own on the dance floor.

Errol loved a challenge. He took the radio to work with him. He still had his moves, but he wanted to prepare, so he got one of the younger men on the shift to show him the latest moves that were in. Errol had to laugh when the young man started flapping his arms like chicken wings and vibrating his legs from side to side; the funky chicken he called it.

"Your turn Errol," one of the guys said. He felt a little embarrassed but he was determined to make an impact at Patsy's birthday party, so he took the floor and put down his moves.

"What Errol! You bad man!" One of the guys said as they all cheered. Errol just smiled. "You ain't see nothing yet."

"Ok guys. Back to work. Enough entertainment for the night," the foreman said, laughing.

Patsy was ready and in the sitting room, waiting for Errol. She had bought a new outfit for the occasion: red hot-pants and a silver halter top showing off a good eye full of Patsy's smooth, honey-coloured breasts. She was eager to go but Errol didn't seem to be ready. For a man, he was taking a long time to get dressed. Usually it was he hurrying them up.

"Uncle Errol! What you doing, putting on makeup or what?" Patsy called.

"Give a man a chance nuh! A man's got to do what a man's got to do." Errol shouted from the bedroom.

"I'll remind you of that next time you are rushing us out of the bedroom," She replied. The scent of Brut entered the sitting room before Errol, intoxicating Patsy. Then Errol waltzed out in slow motion, as if there was a room full of spectators waiting for his entrance. Then he posed as if for a camera, smiling at Patsy, his teeth sparkling like the sun on a river. He was wearing a brand new red Ben Sherman shirt, two tone trousers that seemed to change colours in the light and the latest shoes from Toppers in Carnaby Street, West End. Errol took care with his appearance and always bought good quality clothes and shoes. But Patsy had never seen him dressed like this. He looked even younger than his thirty seven years.

"What Uncle! You, you, you..." Patsy could not find the right words. She wanted to say he looked sexy and handsome, but she stopped her words. This was her uncle.

A short drive took them to the old refurbished building on Old Street. The music could be heard from a distance. People were already making their way inside. Errol found a parking space not too far away. Then they headed for the entrance where a group of her friends were waiting for her.

"Patsy who is this? You never said you had a boyfriend!" One of her friends said, eyeing Errol up and down.

"He is my birthday present sent from heaven!" Patsy said and winked.

"Well, it's my birthday soon. I hope heaven's got one all wrapped up and waiting for me!" another one said.

They all greeted Errol as Patsy introduced them. Errol was beaming. He felt like a youthman again. Errol got together with workmates whenever they got the chance for a game of dominoes or occasionally a birthday party in someone's house. Bee was not the party type at all and he could not remember the last time he went to a proper party at a club.

A special section of the club was reserved for them. Patsy had invited about thirty of her closest friends. There was a big cake on the table with red and white balloons hanging from the ceiling. Ten bottles of wine and three bottles of Champagne stood on the table. They popped open the wine, toasted Patsy and headed for the dance floor. Errol stayed in the corner sipping his wine and just looking on. They all seemed so young compared to him. He felt a little out of place. So much had changed since his clubbing days: the music, the dress, the boldness of these youngsters. He used to love going dancing but since he met Bee, he had settled for just a few nights with mates. He didn't mind spending his nights off in nestled in Bee's warm bosom.

One of the guys in the group came over to Errol.

"So you not dancing man? Why you a sit down and let good music waste so!" One of the young guys asked Errol.

"I got shrapnel in my legs man. From the war."

"You too young to be in war. Come on man. Let me see what you've got."

The wine had taken the edge off and relaxed Errol. All night he tried to keep his eyes off Patsy, but she looked like something to eat, with her hot pants clinging to her backside like a second skin, her top squeezing her breasts, inviting lingering stares.

Billy Jean had just started as Errol hit the dance floor. Errol started warming up with a side to side step, playing it cool. When Patsy and her friends realised he was on the dance floor, they gave a big cheer, spurring him on. With wine and the music flowing through him, Errol loosened up with some funky chicken moves on the next track. He had been practicing and was feeling the vibes. He was all over the dance floor, showing off his moves. It was as if his feet were on fire; had a mind of their own. The music slowed down as the DJ started on the lovers rock. Errol was in his element, breaking out more moves. Patsy could not believe her eyes. Her uncle had some moves there. He had soul and rhythm. When the next song started, Patsy came over and danced in front of Errol, almost challenging him to a dance off. Errol stepped up the pace as they took centre stage, with everyone looking on and clapping. Patsy was a hot mover herself, legs looking like moving flames of fire in her hot pants, teeth sparkling between red lips. They danced, not touching each other for a while. But Errol couldn't hold back anymore. He suddenly took Patsy's hand and spun her around a few times, then picked her up and spun himself around. It was electrifying. The music stopped to shouts of approval and applause. As Errol put Patsy down, slowly, their bodies connected. Her breasts touched his face and slowly came down to rest on his chest. Their bodies exchanged heat. Poetry in motion. Not a word was spoken but they both knew something had danced its way from one heart to the other. It felt dangerous and irresistible, like a forbidden fruit.

It was two in the morning when the DJ closed the party with Al Green's *Let's Get It On*. So every guy grabbed a girl and headed for the dance floor. Patsy came over to Errol.

"Can I have the last dance?" Patsy asked, reaching out to Errol.

Errol took Patsy's hand. It was soft and hot. *Go easy Errol. The girl is your niece. You are a married man!* His little voice kept warning him. But Patsy looked and felt so incredibly good. As the instrumental intro started, their bodies fitted into each other's like the connecting pieces of a jigsaw puzzle. Patsy rested her cheek on his shoulder, her right hand around his neck and the left hand locked finger to finger like a glove. Errol drew her closer, his right leg wedged between her legs. Locked in each other, they grooved with Al Green as if he had written and composed that song just for them, just for that very moment in time. *If the spirit moves ya let me grove ya.* Errol and Patsy were still locked up in the music way after the song ended, both wishing the music would go on, that this feeling, this moment would last a bit longer. They were still holding on to each other after the final notes faded. Friends said their goodbyes and started to leave. The lights came on signalling the end of the night. All good things must come to an end, especially when that good thing is forbidden.

Not a word was spoken in the car on the way home. Errol kept his eyes on the road. Tried not to even glimpse in Patsy's direction. But it was difficult. He turned the radio on as he struggled to drown the sexual tension between them, but the music only intensified his feelings. He was a hot blooded Jamaican man and this girl was arousing feelings he prayed he had the will to resist.

Errol said goodnight. He hoped Bee was awake.

"It's morning," Patsy said as she headed to her room.

Errol slipped under the duvet with pent up desire and a massive erection, as thoughts of making love to Patsy invaded his mind. When he rolled over to Bee, she was a little surprised. She was used to him being spontaneous and often wanting to make love on mornings, when he was at his best. But Errol knew she did not like doing it before church. It just felt a bit sinful to her, even though occasionally she'd succumb to a quickie.

Bee felt soft and warm as Errol rolled over to her and pulled off her night dress. He kissed her breasts, massaged them. That was her weakness. She relaxed, went along. His kisses spread down her stretch-marked belly, not something he did routinely. When he started sucking her fingers, Bee was taken aback. What had gotten into him, she wondered. He had never done that before. He pinned her down and entered her with such force that Bee cried out. He knew she liked it gentle. Slow. Their love making had settled into a pattern, the kind of comfortable rhythm that married couples who had been together for a long time had. This was different. But Bee let go, and let Errol take her with him. Even though it was a Sunday morning. This was an intensity she did not recognize. She could not believe when he wanted to make love a few hours later. Errol seemed to be on fire. He was insatiable, and as always, Bee just went along. Errol fell asleep right after, consumed with the satisfaction that bound them together.

Bee got up first to make breakfast for everyone before getting ready for church. She shook Errol awake before she left.

"So what took you last night, mister? You must go out more often." Bee looked at him with a satisfied smile on her face.

"Why?" Errol asked, feeling a bit guilty but relieved that he had resisted the temptation. Better to live that fantasy with his wife.

"You came back with so much energy."

"Must be that Motown music man. It makes me feel romantic."

"Is that breakfast I can smell?" Errol asked, changing the subject, as images of the night flashed in his mind. He loved Bee. Patsy was a fantasy he prayed would stay just that.

"Don't think because they call this the master bedroom I bringing you breakfast in bed. Come and get it before it gets cold!"

Chapter Twenty

P atsy sat at the kitchen table having her tea, very aware of the familiar throb, the twitching, the small jumps, as if her heart had relocated to that forbidden place between her thighs.

Errol came out of the bathroom, his towel around his waist and smelling of Imperial Leather soap. His taut muscles bulged under damp skin, his hairy chest exposed. Not the guerrilla-type hairy, but a soft patch of curls that made Patsy want to reach out and touch him. That Sunday morning, Bee took the children with her on the bus trip organized by their church. Errol was working a double night shift so he did not go along. Until that morning he had released the sexual tension building up between him and Patsy on Bee, who thought he had just reached some kind of sexual peak in his manhood. Bee went along. Ever since her chat with her friend, when she had just met Errol, sex was something she had never denied him. She did not want her husband going out for something he could get at home.

The sexual tension grew between Errol and Patsy. They played the game, slipping sexual innuendoes at each other until, that morning, when it reached its peak. Patsy, too, had been battling with her pent up desires all those weeks, seeing Errol every day, spending time alone with this forbidden fruit which she wanted a bite of. Images of Errol making love to her invaded her every thought, every dream. Her entire body was speaking to her, in a language she

116

wanted to learn more of and share with him. Errol resisted her every move. She could not stand it any longer.

Errol lingered in the kitchen, keenly aware of the waves passing through them.

"Hm, you look like a peeled orange with sweet juice inside," Patsy said, eying Errol up and down with boldness.

Errol laughed. "Well you should taste my banana. It's even sweeter!"

"Never taste a Jamaican banana yet!" Patsy smiled.

Errol glanced at Patsy as he headed for the bedroom, listening to his little voice of conscience, wanting to resist, but hoping without sending any open invitation. *Errol you is a married man. Go in your bed and leave your wife niece alone! That is trouble man. Any fool could see what going on here. Ah know Mr Woody ruling you damn fool, fool head right now man, but think about Bee! She doh deserve that, man!* Errol left the kitchen wondering if Patsy noticed the bulge beneath his towel - the little jump.

Patsy turned the door knob to the bedroom after double locking the front door. Pushed by a sexual force which she could not resist, she entered her aunt's bedroom with nothing under her dressing gown. She had earlier debated with all reasoning, conscience and morals and thought of all scenarios, especially her Aunty Bee walking in on this act, this sin she was about to commit. But the power of the desire overruled. She was on the point of no return.

Patsy opened the door, trying not to make a sound. Somehow she felt sure Errol was expecting her. The noise of the traffic outside drowned out the little noise as she pulled the heavy curtains to block out the light seeping into the room. Errol was not quite asleep but not fully awake. Patsy lifted the cover and slipped into the bed beside Errol. He was not surprised. He knew, just as he knew he was going to regret this act, which was bound to happen. And what's more, he wanted it as badly as Patsy. He had dreamed and imagined and pondered on it since the night of the dance.

As Patsy's soft, smooth body rested against Errol and her breasts pressing into his chest, he was instantly aroused. He crushed Patsy's lips with his. He never felt such pleasure kissing a woman. She tasted just as he imagined. They were both fully aroused, no words nor foreplay necessary. Patsy opened her door and welcomed him into her rich, fertile garden, which all her life she had been warned to lock and guard, to prohibit any illegal entry until marriage. That place which held the answers to the mysteries behind human nature and creation, the source of ultimate pleasures and pain. But in that moment, there was nothing else. No one else, no conscience, no fear of discovery or consequences.

Errol entered Patsy, hot and pulsating with all his pent up desire. It was fast, intense and over almost immediately. They both exploded within seconds of each other, their groans animal-like, Patsy's scream stifled by Errol's strong hand as her entire body exploded with the sweetest passion. But as soon as it was over, bitter regret crashed between them. What the hell had he just done? In the bed which he shared every night with his wife; in the bed where she read her bible. Even with all the pleasure, it hit him with the full weight of guilt.

"You better go now," Errol said.

Patsy looked around her in a daze. This was her aunt's bedroom, always well made up with her floral bedspread, her bedside table with her things: lamp, bible, hymn book, box of tissue and a framed photograph of Bee, Errol and the children, all smiling and happy. Her Aunt Bee's family. The room, which always smelt of mothballs and lavender, now gave off the aroma of sin! Errol would have to change the sheet. How was he going to explain that to Bee, she wondered. Bee would notice. Without a word, she left the room and headed straight for her bedroom. She lay under the covers thinking about what had just happened. What would happen if Bee found out? Was this the beginning of something, or the end? She had tasted the fruit and she wanted more.

That whole week, Errol avoided Patsy as much as he could without drawing attention. He changed his shifts, went straight to bed, anything to avoid having to be alone with her. Meanwhile, Patsy could not stand it, having to pretend like nothing happened. Errol had fuelled her fire and he could not just leave it raging like that, wreaking havoc inside her. She needed him to keep it going, or extinguish it if he could not. She blatantly carried on with her teasing, walking around in her underwear every chance she had, but Errol ignored her.

"So you giving me the cold shoulder now?" Patsy said to him, one morning, almost accosting him on his way in. "We need to talk Errol."

"There is not a lot to talk about Patsy. What we did was wrong. Let's forget about it. I don't want to talk about it." Errol said, without even looking at Patsy.

But that was not the answer she was looking for. She had fallen in love with Errol. "Look, this cannot go on. It's not going to happen again. Go find yourself a boyfriend and forget about me."

She remained silent. She knew Errol was right. He and her Aunty Bee were happy together. They had been so good to her, done so much for her. She felt bad as well, guilty about what she had done, but she couldn't help how she felt about Errol. She could not just carry on as if nothing had happened. Things could not simply go back to normal. Maybe for Errol they could, but not for her. She had let him into her garden, where birds sang and flowers bloomed. She wanted him to stay there with her, make her lose herself in sweet ecstasy, but before she even had time to enjoy it she had lost It.

Chapter Twenty One

Patsy stayed in her room until Bee and the children left, before going down to speak to Errol. JJ was sixteen, tall and handsome. Patsy often wondered about his light complexion. And she had worked out, by putting together the pieces of information she had gathered over time, that JJ was born before her Aunty Bee met Errol. But you couldn't tell, h He treated both of them as his own. Of course Errol doted on Ceecee, but not to the point of spoiling her or with any degree of bias, which could have been easy given the age difference between the children. He was a good father. A typical West Indian father, leaving all the disciplining and day to day upbringing to Bee, but he provided well and was gentle with them. Patsy always admired that in him. There was no shouting or passing licks in their household. She often wondered how Bee managed everything so well, holding a fulltime job as well as keeping her home in order. She had never seen children more respectful and disciplined as JJ and Ceecee.

When Patsy started feeling sick, she didn't worry too much. She thought she was coming down with something. She felt a bit drained. That was all, but being a nurse, and in contact with all forms of illnesses, her Matron advised her to see a staff doctor. He did some blood work and sent her home to rest. Perhaps all the night shifts together with her partying were taking a toll on her body.

When the hospital contacted her with her follow up appointment, Patsy was already feeling much better. Next morning, she caught the bus and made the short journey to the London Hospital where she worked. There were only a few people sitting and waiting to see the doctor. She picked up a paper and sat down to have a browse through. When the nurse announced, "Next patient please," she looked around, and realising she was next in line, she put the paper down and followed the nurse into the doctor's room.

"Take a seat. How are you feeling Patsy?"

"Oh, I am feeling great, doctor. I think the virus gone. I am ready to come back to work."

He smiled. "That's great! It's good to see you so keen to work. Many of the other staff would find a reason to have a few more days off."

"I love my job Doctor."

"That is good to hear, but let's discuss the results of your blood test."

Patsy sat in silence waiting. She felt confident nothing was wrong. She felt fine.

"Everything seems fine with your test. How are your periods? Are they regular?"

"Yes Doctor. Sometimes they are a little late but they always come." Patsy replied.

"When was your last period? Can you remember?"

Patsy's skin raised, but she brushed aside her suspicions of where this could be going. She never kept track of when her periods came. She didn't have any reason to keep records. Her last period was a few days after her birthday party. Thinking about it she realized it was very late. She was a nurse for God's sake. She could have a good guess what was coming next!

"It skips sometimes. I think it's a bit late Doctor, but I..." Patsy couldn't finish.

"Your tests show you are pregnant Patsy. At least six weeks."

The words hit Patsy so hard, she rocked back in her chair. *Pregnant!!*

"I am pregnant! What you saying Doctor? How I could be pregnant! It only happened once! Just once Doctor!" Patsy said, her voice packed with shock and distress. "What have I done? Oh Lord, no!!"

The doctor's eye brows lifted. "Once is all it takes Patsy."

"Doctor you sure? Can we do the test over? It must be a mistake. I can't be pregnant!"

"Of course we can repeat the test, Patsy, but the results will be the same. These tests are very accurate."

Patsy tried to compose herself. Her hands trembled in her lap. She rocked gently, as the news settled.

"Patsy, it's not my place to say, but I can see this news has caused you some distress. Do you want to talk about it? Or talk to someone, Matron perhaps? You know you have options Patsy. Why don't you take some time to think about it. Things will be clearer once you have had some sleep. Give it some time and come back and see me." All the time the doctor was talking Patsy's mind wandered. *Pregnant! Lord have mercy! Punishment! Must be!*

Patsy left the hospital in a daze. She had declined any form of consolation from Matron, who noticed her distress. She wished she could call one of her friends, but she couldn't tell anyone about this. She couldn't tell anybody. She could not even digest it herself.

On her way home, she got off one stop before hers and walked to the small Catholic Church she passed every day. The Guardian Angel. She walked through the big medieval doors, dipped her hands in the holy water just inside the door, made the sign of the cross and sat at the very back. It was the first time she came to the church outside of Easter and Christmas and she prayed it would live up to its name. There were a couple of elderly people sitting with rosaries, praying, and there was a nun lighting candles over in one corner. She knelt down and prayed. Patsy was brought up in the church but since she arrived in England, either her work schedule or partying meant she had little time for church. She prayed when she felt the need to, but not religiously like she was taught to. She knelt there, burdened by the weight of her sin and the consequence. She reflected over her life; the enormity of the situation. It couldn't get any worse. What was she going to do? How was she going to face her aunt? She had been so good to her. Why did this have to happen? Why Lord? Patsy prayed like she had never prayed in her life. She prayed to Mary, the mother of Jesus. *Holy Mary Mother of God, pray for us sinners, now and at the hour of our death. Amen.* . This was a mountain she had to climb but she was not going to climb it alone. She knew what she had to do.

She dreaded going home, so she stopped by the local sweet shop. Then by the green, in the middle of the square. She sat on the bench for what seemed like hours, until the sun was about to set. The shadows of the houses and the trees lengthened; the moon started the night shift, as her reality cast dark shadows around her. Whatever she tried brought her back to the same spot: that she had sex with her uncle and she was now pregnant with his baby. She had betrayed the trust of her loving Aunt Bee. And nothing she could do or say could change that. Her head hung low with shame and embarrassment. She trembled from the chill and the force of her tears. As each step took her closer to home, it felt like a march to death row or to the gallows. *Oh God! What have I done?* She tried to enter quietly, trying to keep the keys from rattling like prison keys. She tried to creep, wishing no one would be home so she didn't have to face Bee especially, but music floated from the kitchen and Ceecee calling out to her, "Aunty Patsy, come and see! We are making cakes," shattered that hope. Bee's enquiry, "How you get on at the Doctor's today?" made Patsy even more nervous. She answered quickly, excused herself and fled to her bedroom, hoping that she would wake up and find it was all a bad dream. Errol was off that day but he was up early. Patsy was up most of the night, her mind racing with all manner of thoughts of how her situation would end up. Would Aunty Bee ever forgive her? Would Errol accept responsibility? Could she finish her nursing course with a young child? How would she cope as a single mum? Would she have to go back home? It was easier back home. Women were bringing up children by themselves all the time. She thought to herself how stupid she was. She was a nurse. She should have known better!

"Morning Errol," Patsy said.

"Would you like a cup of tea or toast?" came Errol's response.

"No thanks." she replied, as she sat down. She didn't know where to begin. She thought of all the different ways of starting up this conversation, discarding every one. Like someone writing an important letter, then ripping it up and throwing in the bin after reading the words back.

"You know I went to the doctor the other day, Errol." Patsy began. Her words felt like lumps in her throat. Her eyes filled with despair.

Errol stopped what he was doing but did not turn round.

"Well you know what we did. And you know how I was feeling sick."

Errol's hand fell off the toaster. He turned to face Patsy.

Patsy found it hard to breathe but there was no going back. So she continued.

"Well I got the results of the blood tests."

"Well?" Errol said. His friends didn't call him Mr Cool Beans for nothing. He remained calm, waiting.

"What you mean, well? What you think I want to tell you? That I have diabetes?" Patsy lost control. *Why he just standing there looking at her as if she had to read and spell out everything for him!* "I am pregnant!"

Errol was sure his heart stopped; that a massive earthquake just hit and was about to destroy everything around him. Sweat began to gather on his forehead and his hands began to shake from the tremor that piece of news brought with it.

"What you mean you pregnant! How you could be pregnant, Patsy? It was just once! Just one time!" Errol said, remembering how it was with Bee. At first he was careful, using his 'pulling out' method. It took a whole year for her to get pregnant with Ceecee.

"Patsy you sure? You sure is mine?" Even as Errol said those words, he knew he was in big trouble.

Rage bubbled in Patsy's throat as she looked at Errol! She thought of all the men who had and still pursued her. How she teased them, led them on and left them dry. She really liked the Jamaican she had danced with a few times, but none of them had the effect Errol had on her. She was so stupid! Why out of all those men did she have to choose a married man. Not just a married man, but her aunt's husband! Her Uncle. But the way she felt about Errol, she did not feel like she had lost her virginity - she had willingly given it to him! The same man who had warned her about protecting it from men who would love to acquire that sacred trophy! Now she felt she had lost so much and was about to lose a lot more.

"Who else could it be? You the only man I slept with Errol. You think I would come to you unless I was absolutely sure. You think I am making it up?" Patsy was in tears, of rage and frustration.

"My God, what if Bee finds out?! You can't do this to her. You have to have an abortion!" Errol said. He sat down on the other end of the table, away from Patsy.

"I can't do this to her? Me! How come it's just me now! I did this by myself?"

Errol rested his head in his hand, trying to compose himself. "Well we can't fight and blame one another now. But how we going to handle this?"

"Well abortion is a sin. And so is sleeping with your uncle so God help us!" Patsy was beside herself. She could not contain herself any longer.

"My grandmother used to say that there is always a solution to every situation. The problem is finding it. Please don't tell anyone about this Patsy. Not even your friends! You hear me? The less people who know about this the better. Let's think about it for a few days before we make any rash decisions."

"You think I could think of anything else! I am the one who is pregnant, Errol!" With that, Patsy stormed off to her room. *Oh God! Good thing walls don't have ears!* She wished she had kept this to herself, deal with it for herself. She loved her life; her job, friends, being in England. She knew many women her age were having babies, getting married, or getting a council flat. Pushing around bellies and prams, with toddlers tugging at their skirt tail, as if it were the proudest thing they ever did. But she wanted more. She wanted to finish her nursing and travel, do something with her life. Her life. What was it going to be like now?

Conviction tormented Errol as he returned to the scene of the crime. He felt battered, like a heavy weight boxer at the end of fifteen rounds, with nothing to gain from the fight except pain and sorrow. The vision of the incident with Patsy played over and over in his mind. The more he tried to push it to the back of his mind, the stronger it became. He rolled and tossed like a boat in a storm, questions flung at him from every direction. *How was he going to tell Bee? How was he going to look her in the eyes after this? Would she want a divorce?* She had shown him nothing but love and devotion, and this was how he repaid her. At work, he was always the one to give advice to friends and work colleagues, but this time he could not find an answer for his own situation. He stayed at work more, to avoid Bee and Patsy. He worked harder to take his mind off things. His castle had turned into a prison of guilt.

Chapter Twenty Two

Nothing more was said between Patsy and Errol for a few weeks, even though they were only delaying the inevitable. Patsy poured herself into work and thought of nothing else; her betrayal of her aunt let alone that of her own mother. Patsy was alive because her mother had the courage to have her when she was just fifteen! How would she tell her mother about this! She had been so busy fitting in with life in London that she had neglected communicating with her family. She knew Bee sent them news, but it was not the same. She thought of this baby and knew, whatever the situation, she could not have an abortion. Patsy knew she had to decide. Whatever the situation, she was not doing this alone. She had to tell Errol. That Saturday, Errol should have been on the day shift, but he took time off work. Very rarely did he do this. However it was the only day he got the chance to be alone, when the children were out at youth club. Patsy had gone away for the weekend, giving Errol time to talk to Bee. Bee was just happy to have a peaceful evening and suspected nothing.

Later that evening they retired in the living room a lovely, comfortable room, decorated with a collection of various ornaments and lots of framed photographs of the family. Over the years they had accumulated many photographs of the children, at different stages of their lives. Bee kept the room spotless and tidy, and although the family tended to gather around the kitchen table mostly, it was a well used family room.

Bee got comfortable in her special chair, the one near to the book case. There was a small table with a mahogany lamp, a vase of flowers, and a photo of JJ and Ceecee sat on a white crocheted doily. There was a doily on the back of her chair, on the settee and on every flat surface in the room, with all sorts of ornaments sitting on them. Bee was reading a Barbara Taylor Bradford novel - *A Woman of Substance*. Errol lingered in the kitchen for a while, summoning up the courage, getting his thoughts together. He drowned three shots of Appleton Jamaican Rum before he joined Bee. He put on an Al Green record, a favourite of Bee's. He sat on the sofa, across from her. He could not sit next to her for this confession. He didn't know how he was going to start this very sensitive conversation, nor had any idea how she was going to react.

"You remember Joe who used to work with us? He married that Trinidadian woman." Errol started.

"Umhm." Bee didn't look up. She carried on reading, but listened.

"Remember how she got pregnant for one of her friends and how he just accepted that child as his?" Errol continued.

"I remember too well. They didn't have any children together, did they?" Bee asked, her eyes still in her book.

"Well I guess it was he who couldn't make children. He loved that woman like gold. We used to tell him, but boy, that woman could do no wrong in his eyes. Cutting he neck for her! Then she go with the friend and he still stay with her."

"I guess the shame was worse than what she did. Why you talking about Joe? Something happened again?" Bee stopped reading. Looked up at Errol. She wondered why

Errol was sounding so serious and contemplative. Usually when they were alone, he would be cracking some joke or trying to get her off to bed. They had already made love that morning but that never stopped him.

"Bee I have something to tell you that is really difficult. You remember that day you and the children went on the bus trip?" Errol emptied the drink he had carried in with him. When Patsy told him she was going to have the baby, he didn't know how to handle it. He wished she had agreed to have an abortion, even though he understood and respected her choice. He had succumbed to temptation, made a huge mistake, but he was a decent man. He took a deep breath. *Just get it out man. You already done the deed, now you have to face the consequences.*

"Umhm." Bee put her book in her lap and was all ears.

"Bee something happened that day." Errol leaned forward, hands in his lap, head bent.

Bee waited. She waited for Errol to come out with something about somebody at work; something he had heard about or seen. Errol always had some story to share with her, usually something that made her laugh. But he looked so serious, stressed.

"What happened Errol? Something happened with you? Whatever it is, we will get through it together. Remember our vows in sickness and in health, for better or for worst." Bee said, not having any idea what was coming.

That affirmation made Errol feel even worse. He was ridden with guilt and shame that he almost choked on his next words.

"Bee something happened between me and Patsy. I don't..." Errol didn't have time to finish.

"What you mean something happened between you and Patsy? Errol? What you talking about?" Bee went cold.

"Bee, I don't know how to say this. Me and Patsy... Bee, Patsy pregnant. That day me and her...well we were here alone and.... Bee I didn't mean for it to happen. It just happened." Errol cradled his head, as if to protect it from what he expected to come flying in his direction.

Silence filled the room. A chill spread over Bee, covered her with goose bumps. It seeped through her pores, spread through her body, up to her head. Bee sat there in the silence that surrounded them, just looking at Errol in shock, studying him, in a way that frightened him. He was caught off guard by her response. He had visualised all sorts of reactions: Bee throwing whatever she put her hands on at him; ordering him to pack his bags and get out; even a fight breaking out. Bee was generally a calm and composed person, but he expected something to display whatever emotions she must be feeling, not this silence.

"Bee, say something." Errol pleaded.

But the silence grew thicker between them. She just sat there looking at Errol as scenes from her life created a slide show in her mind. Bee had been so busy getting on with things that she had failed to notice what was brewing right under her nose - Patsy's youthful attractiveness; Errol's eyes taking on a different shine whenever Patsy was around. The two of them alone in the house when she was at work; always laughing and joking around, which was not unnatural. Patsy's sickness, the worried look. Her recent absence, excusing herself and spending more time in her room when she was home. Right under her nose! Bee tried to visualise the scene; Errol and her niece. Uncle Errol, she called him. Bee rested her head on the back of the chair, breathing deeply, slowly. Bee's heart pounded in her chest. She closed her eyes and tried to picture Errol with Patsy. She could see Patsy in the scene, this attractive, full of life girl could tempt any man, but not on her life could she picture her husband as a character in this scene. Not her Errol.

"Bee you don't know how sorry I am. Say something nah man. You not mad? You don't want to know what happened?" Errol didn't know what to make of Bee's silence. He wanted her to get mad. He wanted her to shout, curse him, say something. When the phone rang, breaking the silence, he jumped to get it. It was his mate. They were going to play dominoes. He was expected. Errol was the clown whose absence was noticed and missed.

"Who was it?" Bee asked, putting her book on the table, directing her attention to Errol.

"Just them fellas wanting to know if I coming and play dominoes. But I tell them no." Errol stood by the phone.

"Go Errol." Bee said. Still calm.

"Nah. I told them I can't. Not today Bee. I can't leave you like this."

"Just go Errol. Give me some time to think."

"Bee, I don't want to go and leave you alone like this."

"Errol, just go. I said I need to think. But before you go, let me ask you one question. Is this going to happen again?"

"No, never! Bee, it was just that once. It was a mistake! I swear Bee. Never!"

"Then it's over as far as I am concerned. Go play your dominoes."

Errol could not believe it. He vowed never to put his marriage in this mess again no matter who or what.

While Errol was out Bee tried to make sense of the situation. She read her Bible, prayed and asked God for a clear mind and the courage to deal with it the way he intended. Bee reflected on her life, remembering what had happened to her many years ago back in Grenada; the reality of how one mistake can change the course of your life. How her life changed from the day she went to live with that missionary family; how those boys, growing up in a Christian family, could do what they did. How she got another chance in life. She had grown accustomed to just dealing with things and moving on. This was just another episode in her life which she had to deal with and move on. It was so ironic. She was the one who had prayed and longed for another child with Errol. Their sex life was healthy, as Errol and she didn't use any birth control. God had not seen fit to grant them another child. Yet, through an act of betrayal, Errol was granted a child, not she. But she was a woman of strong faith. She truly believed that God worked in mysterious ways. Errol had too much on his mind to focus on the games. He drove around for a while then returned. He met Bee in the same spot where he left her. He took a seat, knowing she wanted to continue their conversation.

"You are a good man Errol. I could forgive you. I have to live with you, and what you have done. I have to live with you. But Patsy has to go. Errol. You hear me?" Bee spoke quietly, without a trace of anger.

Errol nodded. Too ashamed to answer.

"I have thought about every way possible to deal with this. I don't want to hear why, who or how. As far as I am concerned, what is done is done. The future is all that matters now. That baby is yours and you have to deal with it. And we're a team, so I have to deal with it." Bee thought about all the women she knew who were putting up with cheating husbands, knowing and pretending it was not happening. All the 'outside' children they had. She had new respect for the women who were wise and sensible enough to care for these innocent children.

"Patsy will go away and have the child. In the meantime, I will pretend to be pregnant. When she has the baby, we will take him or her and bring up like ours. And Patsy can get on with her life. The child will grow up as part of our family. Nobody has to know.

Errol interrupted, "Bee you mad? What you talking about? How you going to convince people you pregnant for real?"

"I am the one who has to clean up this mess and by God I will. What Patsy did was terrible, but she is blood. I want her to finish her training. Get on with her life. It's best for all concerned including the child."

"Bee, you sure? How we gonna pretend this? I don't know, Bee." Errol could not believe what Bee was saying.

"Leave that to me Errol. Just deal with Patsy. She has to go. You deal with that."

Errol was stunned. He thought he knew all there was to know about Bee, this woman kept surprising him. He thought to himself, this is what his mother used to talk about; the unconditional love, like the love of God. It was the most powerful thing he had ever felt because he knew he deserved to be punished, but without condition she had forgiven him. The two of them sat with their thoughts, not saying anything to each other. It felt like reaching the other side of a dark night and catching a glimpse of the dawning of a new day, bringing new hope.

Chapter Twenty Three

P atsy felt so alone on the train bound for Birmingham, where she was going to stay for the duration of her pregnancy and have the baby. She took the underground to Euston, and then boarded the overground, wishing she had someone to keep her company. Not to talk necessarily, but simply so she did not feel so alone. She looked at families, couples, wishing she could swap with one of the happy ones. But she, of all people, should know that looks deceive. Who knows what lay behind those smiles, what went on behind their closed doors!

It was a long journey and it gave her time to think about things, to roll them over in her mind, thoughts churning like the train engine. She looked at her situation from every angle. Life was so unfair. Look how Errol got to carry on with his life with his family as if nothing had happened. She pondered her future, her new life, as the landscape drifted by outside the window; farms, fields, patches of forest, shrouded by grey winter. Something did happen and it will always be with them. This child would always remind them.

When Errol told her what Bee had presented to him, Patsy it was the best option. She was not ready to be a mother. She could have opted for an abortion and carried on with her life. Ready or not, she was having the baby, so it sounded like a great idea. She was fortunate, really, that Bee was prepared to make such a sacrifice. She did not only forgive her husband, she also agreed to take in his child by another woman. She did not expect forgiveness from her aunt. There was no way, had she been placed in Bee's shoes, that she would ever be able to forgive something like that. Patsy spoken to Matron, who was only too happy to help, and arranged for a transfer for Patsy to the Birmingham General Hospital, where she could continue her training. She remembered the letter from Matron which she had in her handbag.

Dear Pat,

I wish you a safe journey into your new life. I know you probably think your world is falling apart and you are alone. Remember you are not the first and will not be the last to be in your position. A child is always a blessing, so look at it and accept it as one; one which many people are not fortunate enough to have. You are young and strong and will be just fine. You have shown that you are an excellent nurse, and I see that is your true calling. Continue to do your best. I am here and you have my support. There will be tough times and you will cry, but everything is just for a time. Never give up. Don't wish for things you have no control over. Remember, life is what you make it my dear.

Sincerely

Matron

Errol arranged for Patsy to stay with an old friend who had a spare room, but as soon as Patsy was able to, she moved to a bedsit. She could not live with that woman! No way! She was always in Patsy's business and telling her what to do, when to do it and how to do it! No siree!

The bedsit was not ideal. It was small, but it had everything Patsy needed: a bed, heater, cooker, fridge, chair, small wardrobe and chest of drawers, all fitting into the space. Luckily she did not need to bring all the clothes she had accumulated over time, being the fashion queen she was. While others complained about how small bedsits were, she made hers comfortable and loved her little space. She was not the typical houseproud type. In fact, she was on the go so much, she hardly ever did much housework, apart from making cups of tea and washing the dishes occasionally. But she'd learnt to cook from home. Out of the hundred pounds Errol gave her, she was able to buy a TV and a second hand settee, the burnt orange one that fitted into the corner of her little room just perfectly!

Patsy soon got the swing of Birmingham life. She carried on with her training, went to her regular anti-natal clinics and made friends with the other pregnant woman. Many of them were in a similar boat to Patsy; unmarried and pregnant. But she had grown accustomed to her reality and felt no shame about it. It's funny when you know something can happen, but never give it thought or time. You hear the stories and you leave them as just that - stories. That is before it happens to you. Then when it does happen, you start looking into the faces of others, searching for signs. Patsy looked at the other unmarried women and searched, wondered which one got pregnant by a step-father, a married man, a father, an uncle! You could not tell by looking. No one could tell by just looking. None of them knew the truth behind her pregnancy. Just like none of Bee's friends would know the truth that hid beneath Bee's padding. At the clinic, they all had one thing in common - they were all pregnant. Patsy felt healthy and alive. The *wages of sin* were definitely not death. Everyone should get a second chance in life.

It was at the clinic that Patsy met Jean, born in Birmingham to a black Trinidadian father and a white British mother. Jean was almost on the petite side, but that was where her smallness ended. She had the biggest mop of curls and an even bigger personality, a little giant. She and Patsy became bonafide friends. She introduced Patsy to the clubs and nightlife. They went to all the parties. And even pregnant they took over the dance floor.

Jean was nineteen. She was at Patsy's one evening when she came out with her story. At that time, they were both six months into their pregnancies. Jean explained that her mother had had her young, when she was 15. Her mum spent her whole days getting high, and during that time the mum's then boyfriend had got her pregnant. Jean had dropped out of university when she found out she was pregnant. She worked as a checkout girl at Tesco's and spent most of her free time at Patsy's.

Patsy was cooking pelau, Jean's favourite. Jean had brought bottles of Cinzano and lemonade, which they both liked. Patsy had the radio on.

"So where is your stepfather now?" Patsy asked, topping up their glasses.

"Gone. He left when I told him I was pregnant. I think he moved to London," Jean said. She lighted a joint and passed it to Patsy, who declined. Patsy liked to have a drink, but weed was not her thing. The midwives pounded into their heads the dangers of smoking, but she was not going to lecture Jean about her smoking habit. "Then my Mum kicked me out when she found out. Happy family eh! Haven't seen her since."

Patsy tried her best not to dwell on what had happened to her, to put it behind her. She received a monthly allowance from Errol to help her along, but she had not spoken to either of them since that day she got into the taxi, when no one waved good bye. She listened to Jean's story and itched to share hers with this person whom she shared so many other things with, but she could not take the chance. No one must find out. She just told Jean the father was a married man, which is why she moved away. And that she was giving the baby up for adoption.

"What you want to do that for, Pat? You will only regret it. I am keeping my baby. I can't imagine giving him away to some stranger and never knowing where he is, if he's ok?" Jean said, always referring to her baby as "him", as if she already knew it was a boy.

"I know I can do it Jean, but I am not ready to be a mother. I have my whole future ahead of me. I am not getting tied down with a child. I want to finish my training, travel. And if I choose to have another child, I want the father to be there, with me, not me alone bringing up a child." Patsy said this with a deep sadness. Memories of Errol floated around in her head, together with the Cinzano. Jean was always introducing her to guys when they went out, but Errol was still the only man that Patsy had slept with. She was having his baby and she could not forget it. She never would.

Chapter Twenty Four

P atsy went into labour on the last day in December, as the old year made way for the entry of 1982. It was a happy, festive time for many, who were preparing for the New Year: the shopping, the parties, the food. Despite the cold, the mood was warm and light.

Patsy arrived at the hospital that evening, praying for God to hurry up and take that baby out of her fast. Pain wracked her body like she never could imagine. The pain bashed her about and slammed into her body like those big waves against the sea wall in Bathway! Whoever invented the term labour to describe what she was going through, forgot to add the word *torturous* in front of it. She would never again judge the behaviour of any woman in labour.

Her baby girl arrived just before midnight, screaming even louder than her mother. Then, after midnight, when she thought it was all over, waves of hot pain attacked her body once again. She knew it was after midnight because she could hear sounds of celebrations going on in the other parts of the hospital.

"My God! There is another one," the midwife said with surprise. "Come on Patsy, you will have to push again. Just give us a big one now. Come on."

Patsy felt like every bit of energy had been sucked from her body. There was no way she could push again.

"Come on Patsy. Just one more. We're almost there. Come on. Puuuuush!"

She didn't know where it came from, but she summoned every ounce of everything she had left and pushed.

"Yes! That's it! Oh my! Here he comes. Oh my. Goodness me! A little boy! You've got twins!" she shouted.

Twins!! What was she talking about? How could she have twins! Her belly had been much bigger than a lot of the other women at clinic, but she just put it down to a lot of fluid. After all her checks with the midwives, no one suspected she was having twins. Patsy could not believe it. She had never even considered that the size of belly might mean more than one. Not even with all the extra activities going on inside her body, did she ever suspect. The whole situation was too confusing to think straight, so it was with great relief she surrendered, when sheer exhaustion knocked her out for several hours of sleep.

Later the midwife brought the babies, all wrapped up, and placed one in each of Patsy's arms. She had already made up her mind not to get too attached to them but as she looked at the two of them, her babies one boy and one girl, she saw pure innocence. In that moment she understood what it meant for your heart to melt. Their cries stroked her heart. She Patsy, had twins! Was God playing some kind of trick on her? Why would he give her two of them when she was not even ready for one? How would she deal with this situation on her own? Was it some kind of sign? Was God telling her something? She was not a very religious person, but there must be some reason. She decided then, as she held her babies to her chest, that whatever happened when she left the hospital, she would let God take control.

The twins were small, kind of pink with the softest black hair plastered to their tiny heads. She filled her lungs with their smell. She stifled the tears forming in her chest, threatening to spill, pushed them into hiding with the secret of her babies' paternity.

"Congratulations my dear! A perfect pair!" the attending doctor said, smiling down at the babies as he took a closer look. "Twins with different birthdates! And what's more, your little boy was our first baby for the New Year! How about that Miss John!" he said, in utter amazement, as if he had never witnessed such a marvellous event. "A lot to celebrate I would say! Congratulations again my dear!"

That was when Patsy realised her babies were born in different years! Celebrate! What was there to celebrate? She looked around the ward at the families gathered around the new born babies, smiling mothers, the hours of labour pain already behind them, fathers beaming in wonder at what they'd had a hand in creating. She wished she had done things differently. Too late for that now though.

"We'll keep you in a couple of days. Keep an eye on these little ones. They are a bit small, but once they start feeding properly they will be just fine." The doctor told her.

Patsy was relieved to have some rest time and think about things. Let them settle in her mind. But as soon as Patsy got home, she rang Errol to give him the news. She wanted to get this done and over with as soon as possible before she started getting too attached. Besides, she had to relieve Bee, who had her own delivery to do.

Patsy rang Errol at his workplace. She dare not ring home in case Bee answered. She knew she could not deal with Bee on the other end of the line. How could she? What would she say? *Aunty Bee, your baby is ready for delivery*? She had been on hold for a few minutes then Errol came on the line. She stalled, unsure how to proceed. She had not heard his voice since she left. Errol had kept his promise, sending her a monthly allowance by mail every month. Her heart raced a hundred miles an hour. Her thoughts tied up in knots, her words all muddled up as she tried to compose herself.

Errol and Bee had settled into the routine of Bee pretending to be pregnant, which was not as easy as she thought it would be. She even had to pretend at home, for the children. But she pulled it off well. You could do that in England when you spent so much time hidden in coats anyway. But as soon as Errol heard Patsy on the phone, the old guilt returned. By the time he reached home, he was stressed and agitated, wondering how Bee would actually take the news.

Errol waited until they were in bed before breaking the news to Bee.

"Thank God! I can stop wearing this damn thing now!" Bee said. "Boy or girl?"

"A girl," Errol said quietly, feeling the weight of what he had done even heavier upon him. He wondered if this was a mistake after all. That was his baby, the result of his infidelity. How would Bee be able to look at her without being constantly reminded of what he had done? How she's come into the world. How this damn thing going to work?

"When is she going to bring her down to us?" Bee asked, staring straight ahead.

"Bee, you sure you are ready for this? This was my doing. I want you to be sure." Errol said, his voice heavy.

"Well it's a bit late for that now Errol, isn't it?" Bee reminded him.

"Well...It's up to you Bee. Whenever you're ready."

"Well the sooner the better. Has she named her yet?"

"No. She thought we should name her."

"You have a name in mind?" Bee asked him.

"Not really. What should we call her?"

"What about Joyce? After your mother? Let's call her Joyce." Bee said. "I like that name."

Bee and Errol set the date when Patsy would bring the new addition to their family. Bee had to prepare, keep the coast clear to avoid any suspicions. It had to be when the children were out so the baby would be home when they came back. She could excuse not going into hospital with the midwife delivering at home. Was she ready for this? Could she really bring up this child? Bee opened her Bible and turned to Proverbs: 31:25- 31

She is clothed with strength and dignity, and she laughs without fear of the future.

When she speaks, her words are wise, and she gives instructions with kindness. She carefully watches everything in her household and suffers nothing from laziness. Her children stand and bless her. Her husband praises her:

There are many virtuous and capable women in the world, but you surpass them all!" Charm is deceptive, and beauty does not last; but a woman who fears the LORD will be greatly praised. Reward her for all she has done. Let her deeds publicly declare her praise.

Chapter Twenty Five

Two weeks after giving birth, Patsy took her baby girl to London to be with her new family. It was on a cold January day when the sun never got chance to show its face. A heavy fog hovered over the day, covering the fields, buildings, everything along the train's path. It followed her all the way to London and settled over Patsy's heart. She wished she had more time to recover, to heal both physically and emotionally, but it had to be done. Time waited on no one.

She took the first train down and a taxi from the train station to the house. Errol could not meet her as he was supposed to be at home with Bee, who was supposedly having a home birthing. There was a time when parents used to fool children with silly talk of where babies came from: dropped by airplanes, fallen off some tree or left on their doorsteps, anything that came easier than the truth. Jean had looked after her baby boy. She told Jean that her aunt and uncle were adopting the baby, which was partly true. Jean didn't question so it was easy for Patsy to hold on to her truth.

All the way there and back, while her baby girl slept in her arms, Patsy's mind raced with doubts and worries. Not for the welfare of her baby, Patsy had no reason to think her aunt could be anything but the sweet, kind and loving person she had come to know. And she had tried to convince herself that her daughter would have a much better life with her new family: her father, her new mummy, her big brother JJ and her sister Ceecee, who had always pestered her mother about a baby sister. God worked in mysterious ways, Bee always said. They were much better able to provide for her daughter. But was she doing the right thing? How was Bee going to deal with bringing up a baby from her husband's unfaithfulness? How could any woman? There were so many stories of children being ill treated in situations like this. What was Bee going to see every time she looked at the baby? Every time she held her, fed her, washed her? Every time the baby cried and woke her up at nights or fretted her. How was Bee going to deal with it? Her only consolation was that her baby had her real father. And Errol was a good father.

With one baby delivered, Patsy still had to decide what she was going to do about her son. She had not told Errol about him. She had not told anyone. She kept that little secret to herself. She wanted to name him after his father. She called him Rawle, which sounded a bit like his father's name. Patsy kept him on the bed with her most of the times, but at nights she placed him in his little basket next to her bed. He was so tiny, but feeding well, and he slept most of the time. He slept so much, often Patsy had to check he was still breathing. Sometimes she just sat on the bed and just looked at him: the rise and fall of his little chest with each breath; the twitching of his eyes and the corners of his mouth, smiling in his sleep. He was so sweet, so pure and delicate. She sometimes picked him up while he still slept, to shower him with kisses, to hold him against her swollen breasts and give him all the love she could while she had him. During those moments, Patsy's heart ached so much she was sure she could not give him away.

Jean came around a lot with her own son, born three weeks before Rawle. He was a big, happy baby and Jean was a natural. She adapted to motherhood like she did most things. Patsy felt so lucky to have Jean as a friend - two young mothers, sharing and exchanging experiences and learning together. Jean knew Patsy was thinking about giving up her other baby. It was not her place to tell Patsy what to do, but as her friend she held onto the hope that as time went by, and Patsy bonded with the baby, she would change her mind.

"But you will get help, Patsy! You could get a council flat. There is one available near to me. Imagine living next door to each other, bringing up our boys together. Going to school together, best friends! Think about it Patsy"

And Patsy thought about it. She could think about nothing else. Jean grew up in the system. She knew it well and used it well. She had no qualms about doing it. It was their system, their scene. Patsy had grown used to images of that scene; young single mothers on benefits, living in council flats, pushing bellies and prams in front of them and all sense of pride and dignity behind them. No daddies in the picture. No jobs. Everyone was listening to Birmingham's pride, *UB40*, but did they even realise where their name came from: how fitting the name was because all of the members were filling out their *Unemployment Benefit Forms: UB40s.* Or that UB40's iconic "*I Am a One in Ten*" was inspired by the rate of unemployment that existed in Birmingham. Patsy did not want to belong to that "scroungers society" as it had been labelled by the system. She was only twenty years old. She had an accidental pregnancy yet she did not want to become a statistical reminder. A number on a list. A stereotype! She wanted to go back to work, qualify as a nurse, make something of herself- not join the *'pram face'* clan *on a street that has no trees.*

So five months later, with money she had saved from Errol's allowance and her susu hand, Patsy was on a plane to Grenada.

Chapter Twenty Six

Patsy arrived at Pearls Airport late in the evening, tired and anxious. It was a long trip and she was so relieved that Rawle slept through most of it. He was such a quiet baby, reserving any fuss and fret only to alert his mother of hunger or discomfort. He was growing so fast, his little body filling out with baby-soft chubbiness, making him irresistible to loads of cuddles and showers of kisses. It was so difficult for Patsy not to get attached to him. She had tried, at first, to give him as little attention as possible, resisting the compulsion to pick him up every time he made the slightest fuss. But all she had to do was look into his little face, eyes like his father's staring into hers. She could not help holding him every chance she got.

It was a short ride from the airport to Grenville. The taxi driver knew where Patsy was going. Everybody knew Slim. Patsy sat quietly in the back seat with her baby, thankful it was getting dark and praying that nobody would recognise her. Rawle was awake, making little baby noises in her arms. Patsy blinked back the tears that were threatening to surface. She would miss those little noises. They did something to her heart that only a mother could feel the fullness of, and understand.

"So you on holiday young lady?" the taxi driver asked, trying to make conversation.

"Yes, visiting friends," Patsy said, not wanting to get into any long conversation.

"So who is you family?" Everybody knew everybody on the island. He might know her father or mother.

"They from town. You wouldn't know them," Patsy told him. She did not want to talk about her family. The last thing she wanted was for him to start telling everybody how so and so daughter was back with a baby that nobody knew she had. She could not risk her parents finding out. They could not know. She knew Bee would not disclose the truth to her brother about the baby she was bringing up as her own. It was not a normal situation, to say the least. What happened was scandalous! What would her parents' reaction be if Patsy turned up unannounced at their front door with a baby they knew nothing about? Would they understand? Would they agree to take him? But Patsy knew that would not work. That would only expose her secret and bring shame to her family.

Patsy had never been to Slim's house, but she knew it would not be hard to find. Everybody knew Slim. Even if you didn't know she was nick-named Slim, you only had to look upon her tall, thin frame and the name would slip out from your mouth with the ease of a sapodilla seed. Slim lived with her mother in a big old four bedroom house, which the mother inherited from a Canadian family she had worked with for several years. When the family lost their daughter in a car accident, devastated and heartbroken, they returned to Canada, to be closer to their four year old granddaughter. Over the years, the house had deteriorated into a state of disrepair, with broken windows, rotting board, but they did not get wet when it rained and it was comfortable.

It was dark by the time they arrived at the house. Slim was in the yard with another woman and some children roasting corn. That smell was so welcoming to Patsy, the scene so familiar!

"Well ah reach in good time," the driver called out. "Ah stay all in Pearls and smell that corn roasting! Slim, ah bring somebody for you girl."

"You bring somebody for me! Who somebody? I not expecting nobody." Slim answered.

The children ran up to the car, curious.

"Children, all you come back here. All you too fass!" she shouted. "May, watch the corn for me, let me see who come there, you hear." Slim said to her. She wiped her hands on the old towel she had slung over her shoulder and walked to the front of the yard.

Patsy stood there with Rawle in her arms while the driver carried her cases to the house, watching Slim approach her, anxiously waiting for the reaction.

"Lawd have mercy! Well look at me crosses nuh! Patsy?"

To say Slim was surprised is making light of the situation. Since Patsy left the island, Slim had not heard from her, now there she was standing in her yard with a baby!

"Patsy! You never say you was coming! Aa. Come inside. Come inside before the chile ketch cold you hear. Let me go and wash me hands. Lawd. Girl just so you nearly give me heart failure there, oui! What kind of surprise is that? But ah glad to see you! Come. Come let me see you good! And when you make that chile?" Slim did not give Patsy a chance to get a word in, so she just waited until they were inside and settled. Slim and Patsy had met at a dance. They both loved to party and that's how they became friends. Slim was four years older than Patsy but she had the kind of looks that defied aging. You could not tell she had four children by looking at her. That night, after they finished eating their roasted corn and the children had their supper, Slim moved the oldest, her twelve year old daughter, into the room with the other three children so Patsy could use her room. Slim had her children under good manners and brought them up straight as arrows, even though there was no father around. Thank God her daughter was a clean, tidy girl. All Slim had to do was change the sheets. The bed was small, so she was glad she still had that old crib which came with the house. All the furniture in the house was old but it was good strong furniture, and they were lucky to have a house with all that space, as old as it was.

Slim and her mother listened to Patsy's predicament. Patsy told them her story, leaving out all the parts she needed to keep secret. Grenada is a small place and people talked. She did not want to complicate the matter or invite judgement. Her pregnancy was accidental. That was true. She could not keep the baby in England, as she needed to finish her training and wanted to make a better life for herself and her son. His father was not in her life, and she could not bring up a baby on her own and work at the same time. Patsy had thought about it a lot and worked out in her head how this plan of hers was going to work. Slim already had two children with no fathers in the picture. Patsy did not realize there had been two more additions to the family. But she was sure Slim would agree. It was not uncommon for babies to be brought back to the West Indies to be brought up by grandparents and other relatives and friends, and Patsy knew the money she would send each month would help the family.

The night was quiet, except for the night noises of creaking boards and crackling roof of the old house, and crickets and frogs outside in the bushes. Slim's mother had fallen asleep on the chair. She was exhausted from a full day in the market, selling her short crops which she planted around the house. Patsy had settled the baby in bed after his last bottle.

Slim listened to Patsy's story, and knew straight away that Patsy was hiding something. Patsy was not telling the whole story. She could understand Patsy getting pregnant by accident and not being able to handle the child on her own and all that. She had only been in England about two years. But she was sure Patsy had an Aunt over there. How come her Aunt could not help her? Patsy was holding something back. Ok. Well maybe her Aunt could not help, but what about Patsy's mother and father? She knew people overseas made children all the time and brought them back for their parents so they could live their dream and help those at home to better their lives. She thought of herself and her own life, of her own dreams of travelling abroad one day. All about her mistakes and her disappointments with men. How her life was just about struggling to survive and care for her four children with very little help from their fathers. She did odd jobs, washing and cleaning house and helping her mother in the market, but she hardly got any help from her children's fathers. She was her mother's only child and did not know who her father was. Thank God for her mother. But she thought about the money which Patsy would send every month: a regular income. She already had four mouths to feed, what was one more? And her daughter was old enough now to help her with the younger ones. Perhaps she could finally even send her to get some extra lessons. She was doing well in school and Slim wanted her to be a teacher. Maybe one day Patsy could help her to go to England too. But Slim could not help that question which burned her lips.

"So how come you en bring him for you mother?" Slim asked.

"Slim you know how it is. Me father work so hard to send me away to study nursing! All me life me mother preaching in me head about getting pregnant before I get married! I could never let them know I make child already, before I even finish me training!" All the time Patsy was planning in her head, she did not for one minute think that it might not work, but that question threw her off a bit and she started to worry.

It was not a hard decision to make. It was not uncommon for people to take in and bring up other people's children like their own. So after two weeks of eating roast corn, mangoes and everything in season and spending time with her son, Patsy headed back to England, leaving her son with people he would grow up with as his family.

Chapter Twenty Seven

Patsy met Danny at a UB40 concert at the Odeon in August 1981. He was a mate of Jean's boyfriend and they were introduced at the club where they met up before going to the concert. It was a kind of double date. Patsy and Jean went to lots of parties and had met several men, whom she had good fun dancing with, but until Danny, she had not become attached to any. She had learned to leave on the dance floor at the clubs or house parties, what they had shared there. Many of them were married men anyway, looking for some fun outside their homes, and she was not going to make that mistake again.

Perhaps it was something about Danny's likeness to Errol which attracted her to him. He had similar complexion - just a tad darker than Errol's. The colour of half-dried coconuts. He had a strong physique, well formed muscles from his job as a porter and a broad toothy smile ,his gold crown sparkling every time he smiled. His easy charm and ready conversation made them hit it off that night. And it's not as if Patsy were still in love with Errol, but memories of him still lingered with her. He was her first lover, and the father of her children after all. And Danny reminded her a lot of Errol, but it was more than that.

Over the years, Errol kept in touch with her occasionally with news of Joyce, sending her photographs taken on birthdays, Christmas or other occasions. He and Bee even had two more children. It seemed as though during the padding up with her pretence pregnancy, Bee's womb softened and yielded with fertility, becoming receptive to two more pregnancies. God worked in mysterious ways indeed. After several years of not being able to conceive and thirteen months after Patsy delivered Joyce to them, Bee and Errol had a son. Three years later, they had another. Only God knew the reason why he waited that long to bless Bee with more children. She believed there was always a reason for things. Perhaps God needed to better prepare her, not that she had not already learned so much from the time He took away her mother, then cast a child upon her before she even had a chance to fulfil her childhood. He had more in store for Bee, lessons of forgiveness, acceptance and tolerance, which reinforced the strength of her faith in Him. With three children under the age of five, Bee had to give up work for a while. And although a bit in shock, Errol was quite proud to proclaim his virility, which was the talk at work. He was a very good provider. They were both very sensible with their savings and managing comfortably. And luckily, they had enough space. JJ was working but still at home. Ceecee was a lively teenage and a great help with her younger siblings. No one was the wiser about Joyce's true biological mother, and to everyone they were just a normal family.

That summer night was made just for a concert. It was one of those bright till late kind of nights that Patsy loved so much about England. When the air was warm and inviting, the skies lit with stars and people shed their woollies. They took well needed breaks from their tellies and took themselves off to pubs and parks. A night when it was warm enough to perhaps chance leaving your coat at home.

That night, Patsy and Danny grooved under the stars, with thousands of fans, to UB40's cool, laid back, reggae inspired hits. These songs were not written to invite or entice romantic notions, but songs charged with social and political messages. However the vibe was right and Danny held Patsy in a tight squeeze as they rocked to *Dream A Lie, The Earth Dies Screaming.* Breeze could not pass between them as they swayed in slow motion, ignoring the lyrics, taking it really slow with UB40's encored *Don't Slow Down.* And that night, something sparked between them. Something much stronger and brighter than the gold crown in Danny's mouth.

Patsy soon moved out of her bedsit and in with Danny, who lived by himself. He was Jamaican born and moved to England when he was fourteen. He and Patsy got on well and had so much in common, especially their love for socialising. Patsy was an excellent nurse and worked as hard as she partied. She kept in touch with Slim and her family back in Grenada, sending monthly postal orders to Slim as promised, and as often as she could, to her parents. Slim kept her side of the promise, keeping the secret about Rawle's birth mother safely between them.

When Patsy discovered the cause of the continuous discomfort in her left breast, she had just assumed it was hormonal issues and didn't bother about getting checked. Since having the twins, her periods had become a bit irregular and her breasts normally felt quite lumpy anyway. Although she worked in a hospital, she kept putting off getting checked, until she began to feel unwell and the pain was unbearable. An examination detected a lump. Further investigations determined Patsy's diagnosis and the extreme extent at which the cancer had spread. Patsy was in shock when the doctor explained her situation. But she kept it to herself, just like the knowledge of her short lived affair with Errol and their secret twins. She did not even tell Jean, her best friend. She kept her illness to herself for as long as she could, until Danny noticed her rapid weight loss and pressed her to tell him what was going on.

They both had that evening off, which was rare, so they were spending it at home. Danny cooked oxtail and rice and peas, which was Patsy's favourite Jamaican meal, but Patsy did not have the usual two helpings. She looked worried and distracted and Danny thought it was a good time to get her to talk.

"Pat, you going tell me what bothering you? You not yourself these days. This is the first time in all the four years we together you nah lick your plate and go back fee more food!" Danny turned down the telly and turned to face Patsy.

"Almost five years. Five years in August, remember?" Patsy said, looking at Danny as she tried to organize the words in her head. Telling him about the cancer would be easier. But how will she explain keeping her secret from him for five years? "Well I better tell you everything now, Danny. I cannot keep it to myself any longer."

"What you talking about Pat. You sick?" Danny asked. "Pat, you know you can tell me anything." Danny said.

"I have some bad news Danny, but I was waiting for the right time."

"The right time to tell me what, Pat?"

"I have breast cancer, Danny. My doctor found a lump in my breast."

"You have what? Pat how long you know that?" Danny turned off the telly and looked Patsy in the face.

"Well I knew something was wrong for a while now, but I never thought..." Patsy didn't get to finish.

"Pat, what you mean you never thought. You're a nurse, man! Chaw!"

159

"I just didn't think it was something to worry about. I have been trying to work up the courage to tell you, but I still can't believe it for myself Danny!"

"How bad it spread then?"

"I don't know. They have to do some more tests." Patsy lied. She already had all the tests and scans and knew that it had gone too far; that even removal of the breast would not save her. She had not even come to terms with the news herself. She did not want to believe it and still prayed that it was a mistake, that her doctor would call her into his office and tell her he was wrong, that she was ok.

"What are they going to do, Pat? They have to remove your breast?" Danny stood up and sat down again.

" Danny I don't know! I don't know! That is one problem but I have something else I need to tell you. I think I better tell you now, get it all out before it's..."

"Before it's what Pat? What else you have to tell me?"

Five years together and Patsy had never uttered a word to Danny. Not a single day had passed without thinking about her children, living a lie which she was reminded of every time she thought she was pregnant. It always turned out to be a delayed period. God was either still playing tricks with her or still punishing her? She had hidden all those photographs of Joyce which Errol sent her and had explained Rawle as her godchild back in Grenada. That was easy. No suspicions there. No reason for it.

That evening, Patsy offloaded the burden she had been carrying around for so long. She lay it out on the table in front of Danny, like a hand of cards, and waited for his reaction. She had a new burden and wanted no secrets between them. Telling Danny made it easier, lighter, like offloading a bucket of wet cocoa after the long journey from the mountain. She waited for his reaction to see what he was going to do with the hand he was dealt.

Danny took Patsy's hand. He was no romantic, but he had loved Patsy from the moment they met. They had something good together. They had not bothered with marriage. They were OK together as they were, and neither Danny nor Patsy ever brought up the subject. She was not like other women he knew. She was lively, funny and liberal. She loved life and did not dwell on things. He was frightened. He thought she was going to tell him she met someone else, that she was leaving him. These things happened all the time. But this news, which Patsy thought would be the hardest for him to digest, was easy. Her past was her past. What happened before they met had no bearings on their present life, but would definitely affect their future. In a good way, he hoped.

"I thought of telling you many times Danny, but I had kept it buried for so long, I thought better let sleeping dogs lie."

"Pat, my father left my mother with two children and she never saw him again. My mother left us with we granny when I was five years old. My sister was three. Why you feel you couldn't tell me that? Things happen to all of us Pat! You think me a saint?"

"So you forgive me?" Patsy asked him.

"What's to forgive Pat? Having children? The only thing I could not forgive is if you told me you're not a woman but a man," Danny said, jokingly. "Pat, you nah see? It was meant to be. See how God never give us any children. There's nothing to forgive. You have to thank God you never get rid of them, man! What happened, happened. You were young and you did what you had to do. Now we must deal with this damn cancer thing, man! Whatever we have to do. I don't want to lose you Pat." Danny pulled Pasty into him.

She was more than just his woman, she was his best friend too. Hugged her a bit too tight. She winced as her breast pressed into him.

"This thing is serious Pat? You in pain?" Danny asked, easing away from her.

Patsy was in tears, and it was not from the pain in her breast. She leaned into Danny's shoulder, his arm stretched around her shoulders. All those nights she had not been able to sleep, worrying about having to tell Danny, about how he would take it. Even though she was given a death sentence, in the midst of it all Patsy felt happy. Danny leaned over and kissed her. Patsy did not respond in her usual way. It was not a sexual kiss. She softened, relaxed, let go and let him hold her. It was the softest, sweetest, most gentle moment that they had ever shared. That kiss said everything Patsy needed to know without a single spoken word. She wanted to savour that moment, emboss it on her memory forever. They sat in silence, both thinking their own thoughts, but even more connected.

Chapter Twenty Eight

The cancer did not waste time with Patsy. It gave her no time to dwell or worry about what would happen. It hit her with the aggression of a hurricane, ravaging her body without pity. Before Danny even had the chance to come to terms with her illness, Patsy was gone. She passed on quietly one evening, leaving behind a smile which Danny would never forget. Before he had chance to savour whatever time he had with her, he was arranging her funeral.

Death was a sobering thing. You never really quite understand the impact until it actually hit home, until it stole someone you loved away from you. It's unfathomable how someone can be with you one minute then the next minute, in a breath, they are gone. The breath of life extinguished, like the flame of a candle. Only you can relight the candle, and it will burn again, light up that room again, but that life is gone forever. How could life deal such a card to one of the most lively spirited, fun loving people; cutting her down so swiftly, just as she was starting to mature, to reap the fruits of her hard work and dedication? Patsy was not far away from a promotion in her department, she had settled in Birmingham quite nicely and things were looking up. She hoped she and Danny would one day have a child of their own, but that was never to be.

Patsy was cremated and they had a memorial service for her. Bee read the eulogy and gave a heartfelt rendition of *The Old Rugged Cross*. Her friends came out in numbers to say goodbye to the Spice Girl, as many of them called her. After the ceremony in the crematorium, they all headed to the local social club down the road for the *happy hour* which Jean had arranged to celebrate the life of her best friend. There was food, drinks and music, but no one felt like celebrating. How could they celebrate a life taken too soon. It felt more like they were celebrating her death, and that felt obscene. Patsy was one person who celebrated life, not by talking about doing it, but living it. They would always remember that about her. Danny just wanted it over so he could dive into his work and try to get over the sadness and pain which settled inside him. He said goodbye to Bee and Errol, whom he had met for the first time, exchanging promises to keep in touch, promises which were never kept, except for the odd Christmas card.

Another thing about death: the deceased is gone but life carries on. It does not matter how sad you are, life carries on around you, with or without you. Time is the one thing we know passes for sure. And they say time heals everything, but for many, healing was never complete. So everyone returned to their life.

Danny too moved on. He got married and started his own family. He kept his promise to Patsy, and continued to send money to her son Rawle, who only knew him as Uncle Danny from England. Through their letters and the odd phone call, they fostered a long-distance relationship. Until Danny's Jamaican friend, Tony, who was married to a Grenadian told him about their plan to visit Grenada. This excited Danny and spurred him on to accompany them so he could meet Rawle.

A few months later, Danny was on a plane for the first time since he arrived in England. The flight took nine hours to St Lucia then another hour and they were in Grenada. He saw straight away why Patsy always boasted about her homeland, the Isle of Spice. What a beautiful little island, reminding Danny of his homeland Jamaica, but on a much smaller scale.

He stayed with his friend Tony's family in St George's. Friends and family gathered to welcome Tony, who was visiting for the first time since he left twenty five years ago when he was twenty. A huge pot of fish waters was on the fire in the yard. Rivers rum induced laughter and loud talking around the domino table under the breadfruit tree. Danny felt right at home. He loved the vibe straight away.

Danny kept his visit a surprise, but it was not difficult to find Rawle. On such a small island everybody knew each other. They just had to drive to Grenville and ask somebody where to find Slim. So that Saturday, accompanied by two of Tony's nephews who eager to be his tour guide, they set off early for the countryside. They parked on the main road and walked a short distance, passing several wooden houses before finally reaching the house where Rawle lived.

Gospel music drifted through the open front door ,and a small dog barked incessantly as they entered the yard. A tall, slim, dark-brown-skinned woman, unmistakenly Slim, came from the house wearing an apron around her waist, to check out what all the noise was about.

"Good Morning. Can I help you?" she asked. "Blackie stop that damn noise there nuh!" she shouted at the dog. "All you looking for somebody?" Blackie continued to bark. "Blackie! Mash! Ah say STOP that noise! You en hear? Go in the back now! Blackie!!

Before Danny could answer, she said, "How you look like somebody I know so?"

Danny smiled, realising that she must have seen the pictures he sent to Rawle.

"Well you supposed to know me by now," Danny said, smiling. "Rawle's Uncle Danny from England."

"Oh Lord!" Slim embraced him, almost lifting him off his feet with excitement.

"Thank you Jesus. Thank you Jesus." Slim kept saying, overcome by the sheer joy of finally meeting Danny.

"I am Slim. Patsy friend," she said. "Come in. Come in," she continued, wiping her hands on her apron. "Sit down. Oh Lord! I can't believe me eyes! Let me get you something to drink. You like passion fruit juice?" Slim asked, excited like a child as Christmas.

"I like all juice. Anything you have good with me," Danny said, walking up the steps and entering the small but very neat and tidy sitting room. The boys stayed in the yard, joining the other children who were gathered around a bigger boy who was making a kite. Four of the younger ones were Slim's grandchildren from her older children. The smallest one ran back and forth in the yard, bare feet, bare backed, pants full of holes, a small flex kite flapping in the wind, and totally happy. Danny smiled, remembering his own childhood. How refreshing to see children still enjoying pastimes so memorable.

"Ah feel as if ah know you because Rawle does get so excited when your letters come. Ah does get him to read them for me. You like a father to him you know!"

"So where is the young man, then?" Danny asked.

"He down in the pasture playing cricket." Slim fetched some ice from the small refrigerator she had taken on hire purchase from Rhamdanny's in Grenville; Danny's monthly contribution made it possible. She sold ice and snow ice to the neighbours who couldn't afford this luxury.

"So he's a good cricketer then?" Danny followed Slim to the kitchen. "He told me he played cricket, but I didn't realize he was that serious!"

"If he serious! Cricket is that boy life yes! Morning, noon and night. All when he sleeping, he batting ball!" Slim smiled, as she picked up two trays of bread, swollen to falling over the sides, ready for the oven. She placed them in the oil drum oven outside. Danny handed her another tray to fill the space. There were six more to go in. Slim scattered the red hot coconut shells, minimizing the blaze so the bread would not burn. Slim baked every Saturday, supplying the neighbours with the best bread around. It amazed Danny to see tradition continued: Saturday chores; cleaning, washing, sweeping up the yard, all being carried out early, so Sunday can be a rest day.

"So you bake all these bread every Saturday?" Danny asked her, making a mental note to help Slim get a proper cooker with oven at some point. Although he loved to see the tradition continued, and knew bread baked in outside oven tasted better than any other, a cooker would make their life a little bit easier.

Danny spotted the cabinet in the corner, decorated with trophies and medals.

"All these are Rawle's trophies?" Danny asked.

"All of them!" Slim said, beaming with pride, as if Rawle was her own son. "That boy does win everything. He is a hero even to the older folks around here. And all them young people in the village does look up to him. A lot of them don't even finish secondary school, much less make it to college. That bus everyday to town is a real killer, but thanks to you and Patsy, God rest she soul," Slim said, signing herself, "we could send Rawle."

"You mean, he has to go all the way to St George's to college?" Danny asked. He didn't realize that was the situation.

"Well, is only one college we have in Grenada and it's all the way down in Town," Slim said. He representing

Grenada in cricket and running. We couldn't manage all that without the money. Every day I thank God for bringing you in the boy life, because we have to pay for everything he does."

Danny listened to Slim, amazed by how proud she was of Rawle, as if he were her own son. He wondered how Patsy would have felt to see how her son had grown up into this talented young man, admired by his community. How disciplined and ambitious he was. How would Patsy have felt having someone else take the credit for bringing up her own flesh and blood. Danny was relieved Slim had not brought up Patsy's death. He did not want to remember sad times.

Rawle walked in as Danny was inspecting the inscriptions on the trophies. One of the children in the yard had run off to get him, shouting, "somebody come by you Rawle!" Danny replaced the trophy in hand and both he and Rawle walked towards each other and embraced.

"Uncle Danny" Rawle said, beaming.

"What man! You're all grown up! You even taller than me! What Slim feeding you on man?" Danny too was thrilled to finally meet this young man whose life he was a part of. He felt so proud to have contributed in the way he had.

"You looking younger than your picture, Uncle Danny!" Rawle said, with a shy smile.

"It must be the cold in England that freezes our age." Rawle laughed with Danny.

"I have been hearing so much about you already. Sounds like you're real popular around here. Your mother been telling me all about you."

Rawle smiled and shrugged his shoulders with modesty.

"I hear you're a boss cricket player. I want to hear more."

So for the next two hours, while Slim cooked lunch and looked after her bread, Danny listened to Rawle's stories, his ambitions, dreams, his goals, with the aroma of fresh bread tempting him. Slim brought him a chunk, plastered with butter as soon, as the first batch was ready. Some of her customers were already outside calling out "Miss Slim. Bread ready?"

"Cha man! Now I know why everybody lining up for your bread! This is boss bread, man! Just how I love it, crispy outside and soft inside! I don't want to take away from your customers, save two for me man."

Slim served Danny a big bowl of spicy callaloo soup, which he devoured at the kitchen table with Rawle. He noticed that the other children took their bowl of soup outside to sit on a stone under the tree or on the steps to eat, even though there was room at the table. He smiled. Things had not changed much.

Belly full, Rawle took Danny for a walk around the village, introducing him to everyone. By the time they returned to the house Danny had a bag full of mangoes, golden apples, and plums. And it was time for him to head back to St George's. It was the time of day when birds began to look for a place in the mango trees, the little frogs began to raise their voices hailing the sunset, and the moon rose over the valley.

Chapter Twenty Nine

D anny hardly slept that night. Ideas of opportunities to help Rawle kept sleep away. He thought of how proud Patsy would have been to see how smart and level headed her son turned out to be; how God had smiled on the boy, as the old folks would say. He had the quality to go on to university, and the sports facilities and opportunities in England would be great.

He was up with the break of dawn that Sunday morning, as the cock began to crow and the birds made a joyful noise, welcoming the new day. From the veranda he watched the day come alive with people on their way to church and children dragging obstinate sheep to the pasture nearby, where they would graze all day, and goats to fields where there was more than just dry grass to nibble on, until evening time when they would bring them home again. Although the village of Woburn was not far from the city of St George, it almost felt like the countryside. Tony's parents' house was near to the pasture and the bay, where scenes from *Island in The Sun* were filmed, with Harry Belafonte, in 1957.

Tony's mother, Moms as everyone called her, was already in the kitchen and Danny could smell the saltfish boiling. That almost offensive smell becomes tolerable because everything that comes from it is so damn delicious! That morning Moms prepared enough breakfast to feed a whole battalion! They had saltfish souse, pig-foot souse, sausages cooked with onions and seasoning pepper, coconut bakes, Slim's fresh bread which Danny brought, cocoa tea, and Guinness and milk made especially for Tony and Danny. And if that was breakfast, Danny could only imagine lunch! Pops had already bought fresh beef from the butcher, and two whole chickens, and God knows what else they had on the menu. Food seemed to be a big thing in that family. Since they arrived, Danny noticed that Moms seemed to live in the kitchen. All through the morning, neighbours, friends and family dropped by, always bringing a bag of something - fruits, provision, vegetables - and Moms never let them leave without something.

"Looks like you does feed the whole community, Moms," Danny said to her, laughing. They were all still lazing around the kitchen table, full and satisfied.

"Young man, when I was growing up I couldn't remember a time when I was not feeling hungry. And is not because we didn't have food to eat. My mother had ten of us and my father worked hard, always in the garden. My mother cleaned people's houses. But things was hard. So much mouths to feed! But boy, my mother coulda stretch food better than Jesus and that little boy with the five loaves and two fishes! She used to make quarter pound of saltfish feed we whole family. And thank God for that thing called flour! She used to have to stretch one pound of flour from father down to she last child. And pray nobody pass us when she was sharing, because it would have to stretch even further! So I was always still hungry. That why I love to feed people." And she did. All they had to do was walk up the yard and Moms invited them in for whatever she could give.

That evening, after another hefty meal, they sat on the veranda watching the cricket match in the pasture. There were two teams from the village, with vendors selling popcorn, and ice cream straight from the can. There were children running around and, during the breaks, music blasting. Danny shared his intention to take Rawle to England.

"Man that is a great idea!" Pops said. "In our time when we were sending for we children, it was different. I admire you man! Especially as this young man is not even your son. I wish your generation will do more to help their family like that but I know things different now."

"But young man, take my advice. Just make sure you discuss this with your wife eh. You have your own children to focus on. Make sure your wife won't mind, especially for the boy's sake. Believe me, I know some step mothers who made life hell for children. Better leave the boy in the life he accustomed to than bring him into something that might not work! You hear me! Take it from someone who knows what he talking about."

Danny thought about his family. His wife Zelma was British born and bred. She too was a nurse. They had met while he was grieving for Patsy and she had just split from her partner. She was open minded and one of the most caring persons he knew. She had got pregnant right away with their daughter, who was now eight years. Their son arrived two years later. He had never kept his involvement in Rawle's life a secret. In fact, she truly admired him for it. So Danny had no doubts that Zelma would be anything but open to his intention.

It didn't take any kind of convincing. Who didn't want to travel abroad? That was the big dream, the fantasy of so many West Indians, especially the youths. Everyone wanted to go to America, England or some other big country where the streets were paved with something bigger and nicer than their own country. Rawle couldn't believe his luck and Slim was over the moon with gladness.

Rawle was very serious about his sporting career, especially cricket. He dreamed of playing with the West Indies or some team in England, but he tried not to get too excited and count his chickens too early. Some people, especially the ones who were sent for by their parents at a very young age, didn't understand. They came on holiday bringing things - pretty clothes, nice smells and ready smiles - telling you how big you got, how nicely you have grown, as if growing nicely was reserved only for the ones who rode airplanes and lived in foreign countries. And when it was time to return to their life, they left things behind. Things they did not need to take back, as if these things were so easily replaced. And promises, In many cases empty ones: that pair of shoes you have been longing for or that school bag that never came. Promises made with good intentions, with fear of betraying the common misconception and pride. Perhaps it was because they knew that those back home would not understand their reality, so many continued to mislead.

Rawle listened to Danny with appreciation and hopes. But he played it cool, carried on with his life, waiting to see what happened after Danny returned to England and his family. He was ambitious to make it regardless. He knew of guys who got athletics and basketball scholarships, but cricket was his love. Rawle knew he would make it whatever happened. He reserved his excitement until he received news from Danny about the possible scholarship with a university in London. Then, when the money for the ticket arrived, he thanked God for answering his prayers.

Slim received the news with joy, but also like a blow. She had never uttered a word to Rawle about not being his birth mother. As far as he knew, Slim was his mother. His oldest sister once said something about a lady dropping him one day, but he just thought she was teasing him because he looked different from them. Slim would miss him. She had brought him up the same as her own, eating the same food and all, but Rawle was not anything like her children. He was her right hand. Talk about nature versus nurture.

"Boy what ah gonna do when you go? Who go help me round here?" Slim asked Rawle, but she was not complaining. She was too happy for him.

"Well I en even gone yet you talking like that! I not going till the end of September you know," Rawle said.

"Look how God bless you eh! This man who like a father to you! Thank you father God!" she continued, looking up and clasping her hands as if in prayer. "Every day I does thank God for bringing you in me life! Ah know you go continue to make me proud."

Slim thought about the money she used to get every month. It helped her so much. But God is good. He will provide. And she had faith that once Rawle started to work, he would not forget her. God was an Almighty God.

Chapter Thirty

A s soon as Danny landed back in Birmingham, he wasted no time in setting the wheels in motion. After a few months of phone calls to various parties, and a mountain of forms filled in, Rawle landed in England with great expectation and excitement.

Danny was excited to show Rawle around. Danny's wife Zelma moved their son into his sister's bedroom so Rawle could use the room during his stay, but Rawle did not want to cause any disruption so he insisted on sleeping on the settee. The days flew, and before he turned twice it was time to head off to London. Danny was relieved in a way. Although Zelma welcomed and accepted Rawle, he did not want to cause any friction.

"You know Danny, I see why you so taken with this boy," Zelma said to Danny the night before Rawle was due to leave.

"You watching this big, strapping young man and calling him a boy!" Danny said, laughing.

"Well, pardon me, the young man."

"You know, I thought I got to know him through his letters, but he kept so much from me. This guy does well at everything he does. Did I tell you how everybody in the village love him? He is just bubbling with ambition and ability. I just know I had to give him a chance for a better opportunity" Danny said, his voice drenched with pride.

"He is so sensitive and thoughtful too. I am so happy you did. I can see he will do well at anything. He is one of those people. I do love you and this big heart of yours Danny Gilbert," Zelma said, giving Danny a tight squeeze.

Danny signed Rawle up for a two-week trial at Kingston, which was south west of London in Surrey. They had a scholarship program with Surrey County Cricket Club, and if Rawle passed, he could study at the university and they would pay for most of his education. Rawle was the captain of Grenada's Under 19 team and an all round sportsman with great potential, so Danny had great confidence that he would do just fine and make his country proud.

Kingston Oval was a huge place. Everything was large; the doors, the stands, and the cricket field itself looked a mile long. Danny and Rawle were ushered into a large conference room where there were several other young men of all shapes and sizes, having different accents, all waiting with their parents. Danny and Rawle sat down, feeling a little overwhelmed by what was happening. A man in a sharp and immaculate suit, walked in and took the microphone.

"Good morning. Can everyone take their seats please?" he said. After a few seconds of ruffling of chairs, there was complete silence as he welcomed everyone from all over England and the world. Danny was taken aback a little. He thought it was going to be just Rawle on trial, not knowing it was a yearly event that most clubs put on to discover new talents. Rawle was a little overwhelmed, but rather excited by the challenge, which always brought out the best in him. After about an hour and a half of introductions, rules, and expectations of the young men, they had a break for lunch, then a tour of the whole stadium.

"Wow! Just look at all those trophies!" Rawle said, with pure admiration, thinking about all his own trophies back home. Each one told a story that he was well proud of.

"Impressive eh!" Danny smiled. He had no doubt that Rawle would soon be making his own contribution to this collection.

At the end of the day, the young men said goodbye to their loved ones. Each of them was allocated a local family for the next two weeks. Rawle was placed with a family in Streatham.

Rawle passed his first test, a fitness test, with flying colours. His speed and strength were exceptional. After the first day, he stood out among the young men. The next day it was net practice with the batting coach. Once again, Rawle's technique and movements were natural; his eyes were sharp like an eagle, which gave him great timing. The second day was field practice. He took to training like a natural and he was talked about by the other boys.

After the first week, a friendly game was arranged against Middlesex Under 21 squad. This was a crucial test to see how well they performed under pressure. Rawle was extra early that morning. He loved everything about the life of a cricketer in England; it was so good to have the right equipment, and fields that were like carpets. He was the first boy to reach the Oval that morning and headed straight to the nets for batting and bowling practice. This was noted by the coaching team who were organising the day.

Rawle had read about it and seen pictures of Lords Cricket Ground, but the sheer size and beauty of the place stunned him. The grounds were straight out of a magazine. The pitch looked too perfect to play on. Rawle was accustomed to the bumpy fields back home. He could not believe his luck! Playing at Lords! *Wait until I tell them boys! They won't believe me.* He was number four batsman and designated as captain for the day. As if just getting to play at Lords was not enough, he got to be captain too! As Slim would say, *God watching him in truth!* He was used to being captain in Grenada and organising the field, but this was taking it to a whole new level. This was not just his local team in Grenada, not an everybody know each other kind of team. These were guys from all over. *Take it cool Rawle. You can do it* he told himself.

The match was a fifty overs game and Middlesex batted first and made 312 runs. None of the young men from the Surrey team had come up against such quality before, but they were out to impress. Rawle came in when the score was twenty-eight for two in the seventh over. He was determined to push the score on to give his team a chance eventually. The team was all out for two hundred and thirty runs, with Rawle making an impressive seventy-eight runs before being caught on the boundary going for another six.

It was a good performance. Several of the boys, including Rawle, showed great promise. Over the next few days, practice and matches consumed Rawle, until it came to an end and he returned to Birmingham to await the results of his trials. He was quite confident about his performances, especially the improvement in his bowling skills. Failing was not an option. Getting into Kingston University depended on it.

One week later, Danny handed the much awaited letter to Rawle. They were at the breakfast table and everyone was waiting. Rawle took the letter, closed his eyes, signed himself and said his prayers quietly, just to himself. For him, praying was a private affair. Slim prayed anywhere and everywhere. You couldn't call Slim religious. Her church attendances were reserved for weddings, funerals and christenings. But Rawle was used to hearing a *Thank you Jesus* coming from the kitchen, in gratitude when her bread came out extra nice, or a resounding *Praise The Lord, You are a merciful God*! And when a letter arrived from England, and *Lord have mercy* or *Lord give me patience* when one of her grandchildren fretted her.

So much was hanging on this one letter. He opened it slowly. You could hear a pin drop and his heart was beating like a marching drum. He read the letter to himself, not once but twice to make sure it was what he was seeing. Rawle was a cool, collected person by nature, but overcome by the joy and excitement, the next thing he knew the letter was flying up in the air, he was off his chair, and they were all hugging each other.

"Son, I had no doubt whatsoever that you were going to get in! Your mother must be looking down on you. She would be real proud, son. Real proud!"

Rawle couldn't say a word. He was still digesting his news. He did it! Not only was he in, he also got a three-year apprenticeship with one of the top counties in England with the possibility of seeing the world. *Another step further. Thank you Lord*! He let it all sink as he collected himself, return to his usual calm nature.

"Go call Slim then. She would be thrilled!" Zelma said. She had been observing Danny's evident pride and Rawle's composure. It must be difficult for him, moving to England, going straight into this trial, having to fit in and around a culture foreign to him. She was sure there must be some level of pressure in the midst of such diversity. She thought about the youth in their community, other young men Rawle's age. So many of them so misguided, just settling for a life which seemed to go no further than their corner shops and the benefits office. She worried about that generation and prayed everyday for guidance with their own children. It was so easy to fall into that trap.

"Go on man. They must all be waiting to hear from you," Danny said. And praying for him too.

His timetable for training was attached. They were going to be working in coordination with each other so that training and studying would not clash, but complement each other. Rawle didn't have to start Uni for another seven months, but Surrey Cricket Club wanted him to start almost immediately. He was going to stay with the same family in Streatham, not too far from the cricket ground.

Over the next few months, Rawle established himself in the second eleven team as a batsman and a great fielder, catching the eyes of all the coaches. He soon made a name for himself by scoring high on a regular basis. By the last game of the season, Surrey had secured second place in the league and were in the final of the trophy, so his name was down to play in the first team against Essex. This was a great advancement for him because he had just turned nineteen.

Danny arranged for a large coach to take all his family and friends down to London, hoping that Rawle would get the opportunity to bat. It was the last game of the season and it was sold out. By the time the game was close to starting, the stadium was packed with young and old. Brixton was only around the corner so West Indians were out in their numbers. Danny and his posse all sat together in the main stand waiting with great anticipation to hear if Rawle's name was called in the first eleven. The stadium was alight with colours, singing flags flying like kites. The announcer began with the home team and each time a name was announced the crowd cheered. When the announcer said, "Making his first team debut at number six, is Rawle Johnson." There was uproar amongst Danny, his posse and all the West Indians in the stadium. "Yea, yea,

yea!" They hugged each other, strangers and all. Emotions soared with flags. Rawle waved to them. He knew where they would be sitting because he got the tickets for them. "Rawl-E. Rawl-E. Rawl-E!" The whole stadium joined in, "Rawl-E. Rawl-E. Rawl-E!

Rawle felt like a giant. Essex won the toss and elected to bat first. It was a limited fifty over's game. They made a good score of 270 for 8. Surrey started slow, but by the time they got to Rawle at number six, they were 130 with 25 overs gone.

"Just try not to get out. Let the more experienced players build a score around you," the manager told Rawle. But as he was a natural batsman it was difficult to curb his inborn instinct. He walked to his crease, the instruction of the manager echoing in his ears. He looked around to see the placement of the field; they had all come close to him to intimidate him, but Rawle felt strong and the bat felt large. He dreamt about this moment and he was determined not to fail. The bowler took a long run up. Rawle steadied himself, eyes wide open and sharp like an eagle. Sweat ran down inside his helmet but he remained calm. Then the umpire dropped his hands and like a sprinter in a hundred metre race the bowler was off. He reached the crease and released the ball with venom. It fell short and was rising for Rawle's head. It was a bouncer, but with lightning speed, Rawle stepped to the right and swung his bat where his head would have been. The timing was perfect. The ball made connection with the middle of the bat like a rocket. It left the bat and headed for the top of the main stand. The roar from the crowd was deafening as the umpire raised his two hands. A six! Rawle went on to the end of the game, making 68 runs. Surrey won. Rawle was a hero. There was no stopping him now.

Chapter Thirty One

R awle had been on campus a few months before he finally plucked up the courage to approach the girl he had been noticing in most of his classes. She stood out because there were not many other girls of their race at the University. He had adapted well to life in England, and was very popular with the teachers from the university for his discipline and dedication to everything he set out to do. He remained focused on cricket and his studies, determined to get his degree in business so he would have something sound to fall back on when his cricket career was over.

Rawle took a couple steps towards her, rehearsing his opening sentence over and over in his head. He did not want to sound as if he was flirting, but as he reached her, their eyes met.

"Hi Rawle," she said, beating him to it.

"How you know my name?" Rawle asked, caught by surprise.

"Everyone knows your name. You play cricket for Surrey, remember?" She smiled and her big almond eyes lit up.

"Oh, I suppose so," he smiled too. "So what's your name then?"

"Joyce," she said, still smiling. She had thick eyebrows which made the wideness of her eyes more pronounced. Her braids framed her face. She was pretty but not the overly made up kind of pretty. There was a simple naturalness to her that appealed to him.

"Well, you have a last name?"

"Johnson," she said. "Same as yours."

"Wow!" he responded. Rawle felt a twinge of something strange too, a kind of familiarity.

"I know. People keep asking me if we are related. But you are from Birmingham and I am from the East End of London. What are the chances? Johnson is a common name."

"I suppose it is," Rawle said.

And so a bond between them grew like a beautiful flower. They started seeing each other on a regular basis, sharing their dreams and hopes for the future. It was uncanny how much they had in common, but that only made their friendship easy and comfortable. They were both shy when it came to expressing emotions so their relationship remained on a good friends level for a long time. Rawle, was not sexually attracted to her. And being raised under Bee's strictness and as a devoted Catholic, abstinence was her protection method.

Rawle and Joyce were inseparable, eating and studying together. Every one of their friends said they were made for each other, but somehow, every time they kissed, something just didn't feel right. They both put it down to their religious backgrounds, even though they were much more liberated than their parents' generation. But it kept them from crossing the line.

At the end of the year the cricket club was hosting a big New Year's Eve party. Rawle told Joyce about it.

"Would you like to come along, if you don't have any other plans? My birthday is the next day." Rawle asked.

"Well, I'm going clubbing with the girls. New Year's Eve is my birthday!"

"So you're a New Year's Eve baby! Funny. I am a New Year's baby. Mine is New Year's Day! Same name. Almost same birthday? That almost makes us twins. Spooky!" Rawle he said, and laughed out.

Was this some strange coincidence? "Twins from different parents, one born in the East End the other in the West Indies. Yes, that is really spooky!" Joyce said.

"Well, I was not born in the West Indies," Rawle said. Slim had eventually told him how he was brought to her as a baby. The truth did not change the way he saw Slim. She was the woman who raised him, and to him she was his mother.

"So where were you born then?"Joyce asked. They had spent so much time together, she wondered how this had not come up sooner.

"I was born in Birmingham but my mother took me back to Grenada when I was a baby. I grew up with her friend, Aunty Slim."

"Wow! But that is still too far for us to be related."

"Well, what about that party? Will you come?"

"I was going to invite you to meet my family, but sure. I can't miss your birthday!"

Rawle tried to dismiss the little niggling feeling that revisited him. It crept up and joined the others, like the one that hovered over them when they were alone, when physical intimacy should be almost inevitable. A few months later both Joyce and Rawle volunteered for some DNA testing, as part of experiments conducted for a new breakthrough in tracing family as well as detecting defect cells handed down from one generation to another. These experiments were being conducted to detect certain biological issues. Both of Joyce's grandparents passed away early and Rawle's mother died at an early age. Thirty of them were taken to Manchester for the weekend to carry out the test. It was winter time and the cricket season was over. Joyce was working in one of the local shops on Kingston high street. Rawle got more hours with his part time job at John Lewis in London, which kept him busy and in London. He visited Danny and the family but his life was in London.

They had forgotten all about the test until three weeks later they received news that the doctors from Manchester were coming with the results. Individual time slots were given to each student to show up, but strangely, the same time was given to Rawle and Joyce. When Joyce entered the waiting room and saw Rawle, she was taken aback.

"Don't tell me, don't tell me," she said, teasing Rawle. "We have the same DNA too!"

Rawle thought that maybe it was due to having the same surname and close date of birth. They were last on the list at 5 pm. There were five men in suits and ties sitting on a long table looking like judges.

"Take a seat. Please." One of the professors said pointing to the free chairs. They introduced themselves one by one. Then the oldest one in the middle began speaking.

"How are you doing? Young man I hear you're a brilliant cricket player. That's my sport too!"

Rawle nodded his acknowledgement. Smiled.

"As you know we have been carrying out tests on this new breakthrough called DNA," the professor continued.

They both waited for the news, anxious to hear what was coming next.

"Well I am sure you are wondering why we have called the both of you in together."

Rawle and Joyce looked at each other. Of course they were in fact wondering.

"I could tell you know each other. Are you friends?" he asked.

Both of them answered "yes" together.

"Have you known each other long?"

"We only met a few months ago. Here at Uni," Joyce answered.

"We noticed you both have the same last name. And during the tests, we came across something rather astonishing. Did you say you only met here?"

They both nodded. Glanced at each other, wondering where this was going. Rawle shifted, then resettled himself in his chair. That niggling feeling hovering again.

"We have found very strong genetic strains. These tests are almost one hundred percent correct and show you are related. Not only are you related, you are brother and sister. Twins in fact! How remarkable!

The blood drained from Joyce's face. She almost fell out of her chair. One of the men got up and rushed over to her.

"Are you ok? Would you like a drink?"

A drink? Why would she want a drink? She just wanted to wake up. Surely she was asleep and this was a dream.

Rawle on the other hand remained his collected self. After all, this was a new thing and not proven yet. "How can that be? It must be a mistake. We do not even look alike," he said. And as he said it flashbacks spun his head: sitting close to Joyce and the unexplained absence of chemistry between them; kisses without any sparks; time alone when hands should have met and held each other across the table, under the table, but made no move; that unsettling feeling. And that time at an after cricket party, when he had been introduced to the sister of one of his friends, and he remembered how hot his skin felt and how his groin stirred while they danced. It even embarrassed him a bit.

"There are different types of twins. You don't have to be identical to be twins. We did the test twice to make sure and each time the results were the same. You have the same mother and father. We note that Joyce's birth date is 31st December and Rawle, you were born on the first of January the following year. There's a simple explanation for this, Miss Johnson. Do you see? One of you was born at the close of the old year and the other at the dawn of the new year! "

"What? I don't believe this!" Rawle replied. "How can this be? Joyce was born in London and I was born in Birmingham. We do not have same parents. I don't even know who my real father is."

"We can imagine this is quite a big shock for you both. We would not come to you with this if there was any doubt. The tests are extremely accurate. We can provide some counselling for you. We could not believe this ourselves. That is why we double checked the results."

Joyce was frozen numb, unable to digest what she was hearing. She had fallen in love with Rawle, her brother. Her twin! She too had sensed there was something not quite right, but she had hoped that in time they would learn how to express what they felt in the right way. Rawle was her brother. Her twin! She felt filthy, sinful, as she recalled their kisses and their awkward attempt at intimacy. She felt sick. She needed some air. She wanted to vomit. She was going to vomit. Oh God!

When Joyce came to, a university nurse was at her side. Rawle sat besides her looking worried. Then it all came back to her... men in suits...DNA tests...twins! Rawle was her twin! The room darkened as she shut her eyes, praying she could shut out those realities too.

Chapter Thirty Two

Errol and Bee went to collect Joyce from University. Rawle was waiting with her. They were alone in the rest room where Joyce was recovering after collapsing.

"You must be Rawle," Errol said. "Joyce spoke a lot about you."

"Can you please tell us what happened?" Bee asked. "She hasn't been taking drugs has she?"

"No, no. She fainted." Rawle said, noticing Joyce's strong resemblance to her father. He could not help searching for his match. This man could be his father as well? Was this well dressed woman with the kind eyes his real mother? They both looked really young.

"I think you both better sit down," Rawle said. Bee sat gently on the bed beside Joyce, holding her hand.

"We just got some news that upset Joyce," Rawle told them.

"News! What news?"

"There is a new experiment carried out in Manchester University called DNA which can detect disease that is passed on from one generation to the next, so we decided to take part because Joyce said both grandparents died young. And my mother died when I was a baby."

"Yes, that was my mother and father. What did they find wrong with her?" Bee asked.

"No! No! Nothing wrong." Rawle said, and then explained what had happened. "The DNA result shows that we are related somehow. We not only brother and sister, but we are twins!"

"What! That is impossible!" Errol intervened. "The test must be wrong. Joyce is our daughter. How can you be brother and sister? This is rubbish!"

Bee received the news, digested it. Looked at Rawle closely. Composed herself she asked, "Where were you born, son?"

"Birmingham, but my mother brought me back to Grenada when I was a baby so she could come back to work. I grew up with my Aunt Slim."

"And where is your mother? Did you ever see her again?" Bee asked him, starting to feel faint herself. This was all sounding too strange.

"My mother died from breast cancer a few years later," Rawle answered.

"What? What was your mother's name?" Bee asked.

"Patsy Johnson," Rawle said, waiting for some form of explanation.

Errol broke out in cold sweat.

"My God! Oh My God!! This is impossible. When were you born, son?"

"The first of January, 1978"

Bee's grip tightened on Joyce's hand. Joyce had remained quiet during all this exchange. So had her father. She just wanted some answers. There must be an explanation.

Errol was speechless as he reasoned the implications of this. If the test was right, it meant that Patsy had twins but only brought one to them. Could this be true? All those years and he never knew he had a son living in Grenada. This was all too much. Somebody was playing some kind of tricks here. Old worms crawling out from hiding, to haunt him. The old shame and guilt returned and clouded the room.

No one spoke for a while. They all sat in their own pool of questions. They both hoped that they would never have to tell Joyce the truth, but fate had a way of dealing with things on its own terms. It was a few days away from Christmas and they were all sitting in the living room of Joyce's home: Bee, Errol, Rawle, Joyce, Ceecee, JJ, Rawle and Joyce. The younger children were out Christmas shopping. Bee had arranged it that way. She was not ready to expose them to what was about to be revealed. It would be damaging to them, especially their image of their father.

Rawle sat across the room looking around. It was a lovely family home, with all the comforts, cosy and homey, but he felt uncomfortable. Errol, Joyce's father, sat next to Joyce's mother, Bee. The resemblance was there as plain as day, Rawle did not have to search for it. Rawle was a younger version of Joyce's father. Or was he really Joyce's father? Rawle was anxious, but eager to hear this story.

Joyce looked as if all her blood was drained from her. She could not sleep that night. Anxiety tossed her about all night. She wanted to hear everything that had been hidden from her all these years. If Bee was really her mother, then Rawle should be Bee's son as well. But judging from her reaction, Bee was genuinely surprised. Did her mother get pregnant by another man? Who was her father?

"Can I get you a drink young man?" JJ asked Rawle? "I think you will need it." Bee had already told him what happened. He had always had his own questions. Errol was like a father to him, but he too wanted to know who his real father was. And he was old enough to figure something was not quite as it appeared with Joyce's birth. As far as he knew, she was his sister and that was that. He couldn't help wondering about Ceecee too. There were just too many secrets in this family. Questions bounced around in the room as everyone waited for answers.

Errol was too nervous to move. This seemed extreme to say the least. Bee looked at him, and knew she had to take the lead in handling the situation. Get it all out in the open and move on, like they usually did. After all it started with her.

Over the years she had carried on as she always did. The circumstances surrounding Joyce's birth did not interfere with their relationship. She would not let anything change that now. Or ruin her marriage. Joyce was her daughter and Errol was a great husband and father. She had spoken to Danny and got Patsy's side of the story. But how much should she disclose? How much could she, without causing too much disappointment, hurt and resentment amongst their family. How was she going to deal with this without causing some collateral damage?

Errol was a sack of guilt and shame by the time Bee concluded. Everyone else was too shocked to speak. The first person Bee's eyes sought, was JJ. Questions and anger mounted in his eyes, which held hers. He was old enough to question things; old enough to question his parents without coming across as being disrespectful.

A deft silence invaded the room, until JJ spoke.

"Dad! You slept with Aunty Pat? Aunty Pat used to live with us. How could you do that to Mum?" JJ directed his anger at Errol. "And you accepted it? Mum?" He looked at his mother, more questions piling on that mountain. He recalled those times when he noticed things that didn't add up during his mother's pretend pregnancy: inconsistencies; her not being sick at all, working all through her pregnancy, not even looking like other pregnant women. But those things were fleeting then, they fluttered away just as they had come. There was no reason to be suspicious. He just accepted things.

Ceecee was too stunned to even react. She just listened in disbelief, trying to get her head around what was going on. This revelation was all too much. Rawle and Joyce both tried to work it all out, figure out which piece went where as they tried to put together the jigsaw. Their mother going off to Birmingham; having twins but only disclosing one; hiding Rawle away in the West Indies and giving up Joyce to Errol and Bee. Rawle could not help wondering what life might have been like for him if he had grown up with his real sister, his real parents. Joyce had to confront the fact that her mother was not her mother and that her real mother had already died; that JJ was not her brother, not even her half-brother. Just cousins. And she was the other half of a twin!

No one moved for ages as emotions circled the room. Rawle had gained a father. Joyce did not know how to process the loss of her biological mother, but what a discovery and almost disaster, how fate had brought them back together. A twin brother, with whom she had shared everything in their mother's womb, then fallen in love with! Oh Lord help!

JJ was the first to get up, break the tension. "I'll put the kettle on" he said, and headed to the kitchen. He wanted answers to his own paternity. It had haunted him all his adult life. Who his father was. Why he was so different from his siblings. His mother's age when she had him said much more than words. The realization that his mother might have been raped struck him. She had been through so much. He couldn't upset her more. His questions could wait. He would give her time.

Errol still had not uttered a word. He looked at Rawle across the room, his son. How was Patsy able to keep this secret from everybody? She was one brave woman. He looked at Bee, the pillar of their family. He thanked God for her courage. Her forgiveness. He was blessed with another son any man would be proud to call his own. He regretted not knowing, not being a part of his life, but it was not too late.

Bee knew JJ wanted more answers, but she prayed he would not go a step further than where they were. They had a lot to deal with and she was not ready to exhume any more corpses from her past. That's what happens when secrets come out, they stink up the place and that nasty smell hangs around for a long time. Sometimes it never goes away completely. But they would get through this. Somehow. Together, as a family.

Acknowledgements

I would like to express heartfelt thanks to the following persons who have helped, encouraged and inspire me on this journey:

My four sisters, who have inspired and encouraged me to pen this story, despite my challenges with dyslexia.

Cindy McKenzie- the midwife, who took on this project from a handwritten manuscript; and through her contributions and editorial advice, has helped me to give birth to a story I now feel proud to share.

Kamilah McKenzie, for her time and patience with transcribing my dyslexic, handwritten words into a legible word document.

Thank you Richard for your time, reading and sifting through.

About The Author

Errol Samuel is a retired NHS Driver, who moved to England when he was just a boy, in 1963. He returned to his homeland Grenada following the death of his father. He is the father of two daughters and currently the Assistant Coach with the Grenada Karate Association.

Scandal In The Family is his first book, born from an inner voice which compelled him to write and share this story. Errol now spends his days under an almond tree on Grand Anse beach, with friends, debating the philosophies of life.

Made in the
USA
Middletown, DE